MW01279834

THE
GREAT MYSTERY

TRAVIS SLONE

One World Publishing

THE GREAT MYSTERY. Copyright © 2011 by Travis Slone. All rights reserved. Printed in the United States of America. No part of this book may be used or reproduced in any manner whatsoever without written permission except in the case of brief quotations embodied in critical articles and reviews. For information please address One World Publishing.

First Edition Paperback

Cover Design Copyright © 2011 by Summer Slone. All rights reserved.

For additional copies of this book go to
http://www.oneworldpublishing.com

Follow the author @
http://www.travisslone.com

Library of Congress Cataloging-in-Publication Data has been ordered.
ISBN-13: 978-0-9837448-0-1

AUTHOR'S INTRODUCTION

As a young soldier, father, and husband I was presented with a great challenge in the spring of 2004. My life since having open-heart surgery has been very different from what I expected. While the physical recovery was relatively quick, the spiritual and psychological obstacles have been more difficult to overcome.

With my future less certain than ever before, I felt a pressing need to understand the great mystery of life: human destiny. During my search, I often found myself unable to relax, and wrote the following lines in my journal at 1:32 AM, on one of many sleepless nights:

"The mind chaotic every day,
So hard to put it all away
I numb it with my work and play,
But cannot mute it as I lay."

In response to those restless times, I set out on a very personal journey, in hope of regaining my long lost sense of understanding. I hiked through the wilderness, climbed many mountains, and studied some of the world's most inspiring books. I searched every day for the most elusive of all treasures: peace of mind.

As hard as I looked, I could not locate the answer in any one place. I nearly gave up, but decided to make one final attempt. I laid each of the puzzle pieces on the table, and observed them from a distance. It was only then, as I stepped back from what I thought I "knew", that the fog began to lift.

Within this fascinating tale of adventure and discovery, my aim is to tell two stories. On the surface, I offer the symbolic account of my mind's struggle to overcome adversity. Yet if you look deeper, perhaps you will find The Great Mystery to be more about life itself than anything else.

Should this ever-changing world leave me without a proper chance to say goodbye to the ones I love, my last message can be found within the following pages.

Even the greatest oak was once a tiny seed, rejected by every creature on Earth. Yet look at it now! Standing stronger than the others, it provides shade for those consumed by the heat of life.

PROLOGUE

Outside the doors of a state-of-the-art medical center, a team of paramedics rushed in from their ambulance with a young soldier in critical condition. The twenty-two year old patient could hardly breathe while lying on his back, tightly strapped to a gurney that was headed straight for the operating room.

The young man's frightened wife was close behind, holding their one year-old daughter to her chest as she followed. She imagined what life would be like without her best friend, and prayed that their child would grow old with the father who loved them both so much.

As the paramedics carefully transferred the patient to the surgical team, the young man grabbed hold of his wife's hand and stared into her sweet blue eyes. A tear ran down her cheek as he spoke what might be his final words.

"I'll see you in a few hours sweetheart," said the young man. "But if not, don't worry. I've been in heaven since we first met."

She smiled, but was unable to speak as the surgeon reminded them of the situation's urgency.

"I'm sorry ma'am," said the surgeon, "But we really need to get him into the OR."

She nodded her head in understanding and covered her mouth to conceal the emotion.

She squeezed her dying husband's hand twice before the surgical team could take him away. He knew exactly what she meant, and he smiled in return.

The young family parted ways, unsure of how things would play out.

As the anesthesia gripped hold of the young man's waning consciousness, the light overhead began to fade. The medications quickly took over, and his heart rate slowed in preparation for the coming operation. Soon, his heart came to a complete stop, and his entire future hung in the balance, clearly dependent upon the compassion, skill, and teamwork of others.

Just then, as he slipped into another dimension, something astonishing happened. An unforeseen tipping point had been reached within the cosmos, and the ever-expanding universe suddenly changed course. During the dramatic process, everything in existence was returned to its most basic form, and brought back to the clean slate from which it all began. Not even the light could escape the unprecedented gravitational pull.

When the miraculous event was finally over, the universe had been compressed into a tiny, unrecognizable spec. Such events had taken place many times throughout eternity, and the mysterious cycle of cosmic re-birth would surely never end.

Then, after a brief peace during which nothing could evolve, the most amazing and inconceivable explosion occurred...and like a beating heart, The Great Mystery went to work...yet again.

CHAPTER
1

...some time later...

On a warm and almost silent summer afternoon in the land between the two great rivers, a bare-footed young girl wandered curiously from the primitive village in which she lived. She skipped happily along a lightly worn grassy path, which slithered its way into the nearby jungle. The dense green canopy, into which she traveled, remained mostly unexplored, offering an unrivalled adventure to anyone with the courage, or innocence to enter. The girl's name was Eva, and there was not a worry on her pure young mind.

For the brown haired, blue eyed seven-year-old, the world was not only pleasing to her senses, but also simple to understand. The fruits of her life's experience had left her with a comforting sense of peace and fulfillment. She had everything she needed by day, and slept well at night. No specific thoughts or actions led to this feeling, it just was. For Eva, conflict and suffering did not yet exist, for she had faced neither fear, nor adversity before. The light shined in through the trees by day, and reflected off of the great rivers by night. As the light of the world moved, so too did Eva. It was always there with her.

In Eva's life, there was but one great passion: art. Her passion for artistic beauty and complicated, yet intelligent designs, had entertained her thoughts for nearly every second of her seven joyous years. Thus was the case as she wandered down the grassy path: all the while inspired by the natural wonders of her surroundings.

It was the only path she knew, and she had walked portions of it prior to that day. With each excursion, she had gone further from her riverside village, gradually opening her eyes to the lures of the larger world.

Tempted by the many discoveries she had made in the past, Eva wandered further that day than she had ever been before. She longed for the feeling of finding something new and exciting. However, as she lost track of time, she would soon discover something that would change her life forever. Life, as she knew it then, would never be the same again.

CHAPTER
2

Eva was about to return home, as she always did, when she heard a voice carried by the wind... much like a whisper.

"Eva," whispered the wind.

The voice called out to her again from the jungle just beyond her view. However, she could not distinguish its origin.

Eva realized that the remaining daylight was running out fast. She needed to get back to the village before sunset, but curiosity got the best of her.

With nothing to fear, she took a short detour into the trees, just west of the known path. While carefully pushing aside hanging branches and stepping over thick brush, a rustle in the tall grasses up ahead momentarily startled her.

Eva picked up her pace, trying to see what, or who, was moving about. She contemplated whether an older sibling, or a village hunter like her father, might be playing games, as they often did. *At least that would explain the voice*, she thought.

On the other hand, the wind often played games of its own. Perhaps her imagination had gotten the best of her, and she had wondered in search of a small animal looking for food on the forest floor. Either way, she was curious.

In the excitement, she had not taken notice of the suns waning position in the evening sky. She paused to consider her options before deciding to make her way back to the path, and head home.

However, just as Eva began to turn around, the voice spoke yet again. This time there was no mistaking it.

"Eva," whispered the mysterious voice. The sound crept through the jungle, echoing from every direction.

Suddenly, feeling uneasy for the first time, Eva moved anxiously in the direction of the voice. As she turned, a young boy approached through the bushes. They bumped right into each other, and then quickly backed off in surprise. They curiously inspected one another, but found few things in common. From what she could tell, the boy was about her age, and equally human. The similarities ended there.

His skin was much darker than Eva's, and his eyes were like light brown marbles. The boy possessed neatly groomed black hair, a luxury of which she had never seen. He dressed very differently from what she was accustomed. On his feet, he wore sandals made of fine leather, and on his body an elaborate robe of many bright colors. The beauty and quality of the boy's apparel were in stark contrast to the plain white linens of those living in Eva's tiny village.

Having never met anyone from outside her village, Eva was certain she had never seen the boy before. Yet somehow, he had surely been calling her by name just moments ago. Interested in who the boy was, Eva inquired about three things.

"Who are you?" she asked. "What are you doing here in the woods as the sun sets, and how do you know my name?"

With growing intrigue, their eyes locked on to one another as an unfamiliar feeling descended upon the forest. Eva waited patiently for his reply.

"My name is Amir," the boy quietly answered. "I have abandoned a familiar sandy path in search of a voice I heard upon the wind just minutes ago."

Confused by the third question, Amir asked something in return.

"I do not know your name as you assume," he said. "But why would you ask for mine, when you called to me just moments ago? Your voice was unmistakable."

Certain she had not called to him like he suggested, Eva's pulse quickened, and a new sensation rushed through her veins. The tiny hairs on her body rose, as chills ran down her spine. Having lost her sense of direction during the brief chase, her well-known path was now hidden from sight.

The terrifying grumble of thunder echoed throughout the darkening sky. Eva stared with wide eyes at Amir, trembling with fear. It was the feeling of separation from what she knew; a sensation that was not about to end.

The life giving sun had set, flashing storm clouds had rolled in, bringing with them the familiar scent of rain, and darkness had fallen harshly upon the dense jungle...

CHAPTER
3

Hardly able to see one another, Eva and Amir held hands tightly and looked for shelter. The sky opened up, and rain began to pour. Large droplets of water fell from the sinister clouds, bombarding the forest canopy high above. Amir and Eva looked up in anticipation. They could hear it coming. A mist descended upon the frightened young children, moistening their exposed skin. Finally, the battered jungle could no longer shield them from the downpour.

Together, they searched the vicinity for what seemed like an eternity, but found no evidence of a trail. It seemed their paths had been erased from the earth, overgrown with the same vegetation as the rest of the area. Their eyes grew heavy as they exhausted themselves in search of a way home.

Realizing that finding their way in the dark was unlikely, they found shelter in a dense cave-like opening in the brush.

Fearing they would be lost forever, but glad not to be alone, they leaned against an enormous tree, which served as the backbone of their vegetated refuge. Too tired for conversation, Eva and Amir fell into a deep and dreamless sleep.

CHAPTER
4

The following morning, Eva awoke within a pleasantly calm surrounding. A gentle breeze blew peacefully through drying leaves above. The rustling treetops were supplemented by the sound of chirping birds. It was the recurrent music of nature.

The storm clouds had cleared. The rain had ceased, and the innocent young girl could see her surroundings clearly once again. The sun's light slowly climbed from the east into the sky above. It was astounding how light could alter one's mood so unavoidably.

Having never been lost before, Eva considered the possibility that she may not find her way back to the village. In order to find food, water, and safety before the day's end, they had to get moving. She nudged Amir with her elbow a few times to wake him.

"Come on Amir," she urged. Eva stood up and peeled the fallen wet leaves from her body. "We need to get going. Our way home can't be far."

Amir yawned and stretched as he stood and surveyed the surrounding forest. To Eva's surprise, the boy was wise beyond his years.

"Just as we were tempted by the wind," said the boy, "we must follow the elements to find our way home. Don't worry... the water will lead us there."

"I'm not sure what you mean," said Eva with a confused look on her face. "I don't see any streams or rivers to follow."

"Last night," Amir explained, "as the rain fell into the forest, we too fell into this place. Notice however, that the rain has since moved on."

"So, like I said," Eva teased, "We need to get going."

"Clouds gather over the great seas," continued the wise young boy, "then carry their rains to distant lands. The droplets are scattered as they fall into the most unfamiliar places. Nevertheless, they make their way home. They do this by going with the flow, not by fighting the current. The fallen sprinkles come together, becoming greater as they approach the sea. They journey through foreign territory, as if they had been there before.

"There is always a path of least resistance, and it is there that the water flows. No need to panic, if we do as the rain does, we will find our way home."

Little did Eva know, the seed which one day would grow into a spectacular discovery, had just been planted in her mind. For now however, she simply prepared to move out.

"Well with a brain like that, it looks like I'll be following you," Eva said.

Eva and Amir briefly observed their immediate area, but noticed nothing of interest. They began pushing their way through the woods in search of anything that might help them get home.

They had not been walking long when Eva's foot got caught on a low growing vine, causing her to trip and fall hard to the ground. She twisted her ankle as her body spun awkwardly during the fall. The sudden pain caused her to grasp at her lower leg. She closed her eyes and began to cry.

Amir had been walking slightly ahead, but immediately turned back and knelt down to comfort his injured friend. It didn't take him long to notice the swelling in her ankle.

He calmed her fears by assuring her that he could help, and then gathered some nearby twigs and tall grass. Using only the raw materials, he quickly fashioned a brace, and used it to stabilize the injured joint. While it didn't do much for the pain, it would enable her to walk without risking further injury.

He also found a thick, freshly fallen branch in the vicinity, perhaps from the previous night's storm. He broke off a piece about three feet in length, and gave it to Eva for balance and support.

Grabbing hold of Amir's arm with one hand, and the stick with the other, Eva slowly stood up and thanked him for his support. She could not help but wonder how the young boy knew so much about first aid, but she was glad he was there.

"Thank you," she said sincerely. "I'm not sure what I would have done without you."

"Well, for starters," Amir replied with a smile, "you would not be lost in the woods."

CHAPTER
5

Amir and Eva moved carefully through the forest, searching for anything familiar. The calm that had existed all morning suddenly dissolved, and the tropical wind began to accelerate. The towering forest canopy above began to sway back and forth. Surrounding trees creaked and moaned as their bending trunks were tested against the force of the tremendous gusts.

Eva and Amir looked up, wondering if another storm might be blowing in, but quickly realized that the sky above was crystal clear. Like standing in the eye of a hurricane, the calm where they stood was somehow out of place with the forces at work all around. They stared in wonder at the chaos surrounding them, while their clothes dangled motionless from their bodies.

When the mysterious event finally passed, an unexplainable sight appeared.

With wide-eyed astonishment, their mouths fell open. Distracted by the moving treetops, the landscape had somehow been rearranged, and an unfamiliar path now appeared before them.

The finely constructed cobblestone path meandered into the woods to their left, and to their right. The weathered grey stones were arranged like puzzle pieces and held together with sandy mortar. Short green grass covered the ground between the path's raised edges and the nearby wood line.

Being much wider and more advanced than the primitive trails from which they had come, this path seemed to have been built for heavy traffic. Clearly, this was a much-anticipated sight for the lost young couple. Nevertheless, it was an unlikely way back to the village.

Something was amiss, but they held on to the hope that this new path would somehow lead them home.

CHAPTER
6

E va knelt down to admire the craftsmanship and time required to construct such a beautiful and sturdy path. To her, it was a work of art. She ran her hand over its smooth stones as she dreamed of what the nearby town must be like. *What a village it must be to have the luxury of time,* she thought. Surely, much time, and a certain necessity, had inspired these people to build the stone path.

Where Eva had come from, such time and reason were non-existent. Her family had spent the majority of their time hunting and gathering food, yet they were unable to store large reserves without spoilage. Such difficulties seemed to have been mastered by these mysterious new neighbors.

Having been sidetracked by their recent discovery, Eva had not noticed the tiny stream flowing in the woods on the other side of the path. She turned to Amir, hoping he would have the answers.

"So...what should we do now?" she asked.

"Well," replied Amir, "if you're asking me, I say we keep searching for the familiar paths from which we came. I've never seen this path before, and I don't know where it goes."

Eva was confident that his advice was sound, but could not resist the temptation of finding something new and exciting. *Surely*, she thought, *there must be a village of some kind nearby.*

In her mind, she rationalized why the new way was better. She felt that her simple life had little to offer, and that this fancy path would bring exciting adventure and meaning to her life. All she needed to do was convince Amir.

"We're certainly nowhere near the other paths," persuaded Eva. "We've been walking east for hours, and would have crossed one of them by now."

Amir replied, "Perhaps we should go back. We must have walked over it in the storm last night without noticing."

"No way," argued Eva. "If we go back, we'll be stuck out here again tonight. We should just take this path wherever it goes. You aren't going to leave me out here alone, are you?"

She could see him thinking. Knowing she needed to pounce on the opportunity to bargain, she decided to offer a deal.

"I'll tell you what," she said, "you can choose which way we go. Shall we go left or right?"

A puzzled look crossed Amir's face, letting Eva know that he was at least considering the option. He knew for certain that they would not find their paths before dark.

"Perhaps survival *should* be our primary consideration," he said. "We need food, water, and shelter, and will most likely find it on this well made path."

Strangely, Eva noticed, while the path seemed to have been made to endure heavy traffic, there was currently no one in sight. While it picked her curiosity, she wasn't sure what to make of it, and had no reason to be suspicious.

"Fine then," he said. "Let's get going. We'll go right."

Amir was careful to observe the surroundings and not move out in haste. In doing so, he noticed the small stream in the woods on the other side of the path. The water flowed to the right, and Amir saw this as a clue. He explained his rationale to Eva.

"We'll follow the way of the rain," he said, "and make our way back home. Your village is by the water and so is mine. This stream surely feeds into a larger river. Perhaps even the one on which our villages lie, if not, we can ask for food and directions along the way."

Eva was convinced and ready to go, so they stepped out onto the path together. Each glanced briefly to the left, and then followed the path in the direction of the flowing stream. As far as their eyes could see, they were alone in the forest. However, as they turned to head right, a frighteningly familiar voice whispered to them from behind. The eerie sound crept through the woods, causing them to stop in their tracks.

With shared emotion, they glanced briefly into one another's eyes as they turned to see who it was. But to their surprise, no one was there.

They became uncomfortable by the mere thought of the mysterious voice, and goose bumps arose on their skin.

They paused to consider the possibilities. *Could this be the same voice that had tricked them the day before*? they thought. *And if so, why was it calling to them?*

Knowing the results of listening to the wind the first time, they would not make the same mistake again. After hearing nothing for a few moments, they looked back at one another, wondering if it had only been their imagination. But as soon as their fears had dissipated, it spoke to them yet again.

"Wait," whispered the voice. "Do not run."

This time, as they looked in the direction of the voice, an elderly woman appeared on the path, calmly walking toward them from the distance. Eva and Amir stared in awe at the unique characteristics of the woman. They had never seen her before, or anyone like her for that matter. Surely, she had not come from either of their villages.

Then, with a chilling likeness to the voice of the wind, the old woman called out to them by name. Amir and Eva stood frozen in the center of the path, their bodies trembling from both fear, and admiration.

CHAPTER
7

As the mysterious old woman approached, she was somehow illuminated more than the surrounding forest. She walked effortlessly, as if her age had taken no effect on her body.

She seemed quite tall to the children, perhaps five feet or so. Her olive skin was similar to that of Amir's, though it appeared thin and fragile. Her shoulder-length hair was a wavy blend of black and grey, and though it blew wildly in the wind, not a single strand ever obstructed her face. Her fierce green eyes glowed like torches in the night as she approached.

The woman paused, patiently observed the area, and finally settled her gaze on the children. Amir and Eva listened closely as she began...

"Hello children," she said. "Why have you chosen to stray from your familiar paths?"

Eva and Amir had a feeling that the woman's question might be rhetorical. From what they could tell, it was she who had called them from their paths. The woman's voice had an uncanny resemblance to the sound of the wind. Eva decided to reply.

"I was walking peacefully in the woods when I heard a voice calling my name," she explained. "I left my path in search of the voice. I don't know how I got lost. I was only hoping to find something interesting in the forest."

"And how did you meet your friend?" asked the woman.

"When I left my path, I found Amir in the woods. He was searching for the voice as well."

"Do your parents approve of your wandering in the woods at all hours of the day and night?"

The children were silent for a moment, knowing the woman would read any lack of integrity with ease. Then Amir answered.

"No Ma'am," he said. "They would not approve, but we only got lost while trying to find our way home."

"Would you like some help?" the woman asked.

Eva's newfound mistrust of the unknown convinced her that following the mysterious woman was a bad idea. She already feared that this woman's voice had caused them to get lost in the first place. She and Amir would simply follow the new path back home as planned.

"We're young," Eva said, "but I think we can take care of ourselves. Thanks for the offer."

"Ah. I see," the woman replied. "Then I'll let you be on your way."

The children turned to continue to go, glad that they had averted the strange woman's temptation. The encounter had nearly ceased, but Eva turned back. She wanted further explanation about something on her mind.

"May I ask you a question?"

"Of course you may," she replied. "What is it?"

"Well, I recognize your voice from the woods the other day. Why did you call us?" Eva asked.

The woman smiled, thankful that she had asked the question.

"I call for people quite often," said the woman. "But few have heard my voice. If you have, then you are worthy of my offer."

"What offer is that?" Eva asked.

"There is a secret treasure, concealed long ago, which offers power beyond your wildest dreams. It is fully capable of bringing peace and harmony to troubled lands, and uniting the entire world. This treasure has existed since ancient times, and is displayed in plain view. Nevertheless, only those who seek my voice can hope to find it, and unlock its full potential."

Amir and Eva glanced at each other in disbelief that any treasure could be so powerful. As great as it sounded, they were just kids, and could never find it on their own anyway.

"That all sounds great," Eva replied, "but what's the catch?"

"I will do for you one of two things," explained the woman. "First, if you so choose, I will show you the way home. I am aware that you are lost, and anxious to return to your families."

Intrigued by the sudden possibility of finding their way home, Eva and Amir listened anxiously for the second option.

"On the other hand," said the woman, "if you can take care of yourselves as you say, I will show you a different way home. You will be given the tools and guidance necessary to lead you to the secret treasure. Unfortunately, I cannot reveal its location, for in order to possess the greatest reward, one must endure the greatest journey."

With their whole lives in front of them, Amir and Eva imagined the endless possibilities of possessing such a treasure. To unite the world, or even a village, would certainly be amazing. On the other hand, they knew their parents would be worried sick until they returned. By any measure, it was a monumental decision.

The mysterious old woman waited patiently while they considered the options. Whatever the choice, the implications were far greater than they knew.

CHAPTER
8

After talking it over for a moment, Amir and Eva decided to seek the treasure. They figured that, even if they missed their families, to return home with the treasure would be much more exciting. Never again would the ruling elders look down on them. They fought their suspicions of the mysterious woman, feeling that the reward of believing outweighed the risk of not.

Amir took charge and voiced their decision to the old woman. "We have chosen to accept your offer, and will go in search of the secret treasure."

"Very well then," said the woman. "From this day forth you will be driven to find the secret treasure. In an effort to build trust, I have shown you the way home as well...in case you change your minds. As you look to your left and right, you will see that your original paths have been restored."

Glancing to their sides, as the woman had suggested, the children were shocked by what they saw. Sure enough, starting near the edge of the stone path and wandering into the woods, a lightly worn grassy path went left, and a narrow sandy path went right. Upon seeing this, Amir and Eva were fully convinced of the strange old woman's miraculous power.

"Your villages are just beyond the horizon," she promised. "There, you will find the food, water and security that you so desire. However, if you fail to seek the treasure until it is found, you will bring great suffering upon your people. Their food will run out, their water will dry up, and their villages will be burnt to the ground by invading armies."

Confounded by the idea that returning home would not be safe, Eva and Amir looked at one another, simultaneously having envisioned the impending destruction of their homelands. They wondered if they had done something terribly wrong.

"Why would you bring suffering on our people?" Eva asked. "What kind of person does that?"

"In promising such things for your people," the woman explained, "I have fulfilled my end of the bargain."

"How do you figure that?" interrupted Amir. "It seems like we got the short end of the stick on this deal."

"You ask for the greatest treasure in the world, and then complain about how it is delivered. If you trust that the treasure is real, why question my ways?

"Though the treasure is nearby, it will be very hard to find. If I allow you to go home without consequence, you will give up and never find it. For that reason, you have been given great motivation to search for the treasure.

"Once it is found, you may return home without worry, but until then you must search. Your own decisions will determine the well-being of your people.

"I have provided you with the tools, as promised. It is futile to question my ways. I wish you good fortune on your journey, but as for me, I must be going."

Amir and Eva stood on the cobblestone trail considering where they would begin their quest. While contemplating the road ahead, they listened as the woman offered some words of encouragement.

"I assure you that the treasure will be found. With it, you will find answers to the most fundamental questions of human existence."

A low-lying layer of fog began to form around the woman's feet, and slowly began to fill the surrounding jungle. The children observed, certain that she would vanish at any moment.

Fearing for the safety of the old woman who now held his hopes and dreams in her hands, Amir called out as she departed.

"Where will you be if we need you?" he asked. "How will you survive alone in the wilderness?"

The mysterious woman turned only her head as she continued to walk away.

"Do not worry about me," she said. "I know a thing or two about nature. If you need me, just look around."

Just then, a strong breeze blew in from both the east and the west, creating a whirlwind around the woman. Having revealed her message to the chosen ones, she began to disappear as the children looked on in awe. Her ghostly figure transformed before their eyes, accelerating into a spiral like a tornado on the path. In a matter of seconds, she had faded into thin air.

The Great Mystery... had vanished.

CHAPTER
9

When the wind stopped blowing and the falling leaves had settled on the ground, Eva and Amir could not help but notice the arrow- shaped symbol that remained on the path. It pointed clearly to the north, the only direction they had not considered going. It was away from their homes, and against the flow of the small creek.

In awe of what had just transpired, in fear of returning home, and in faith that the treasure was real, Eva and Amir headed north in search of their reward. They had made it this far together, and it had been the experience of a lifetime so far. Perhaps one day they would unite the world, as promised. They could not imagine how or why it would be, but they had hope.

They moved north together side by side. As they walked, Eva noticed that her ankle was suddenly free of pain and swelling, and her stride was smooth and easy. For whatever reason, she had been cured just in time for the journey.

As Eva and Amir walked briskly up the path, the oncoming stream slowly disappeared. The thinning air grew colder by the minute, and the branches all around became increasingly bare as their leaves fell softly to the ground. The increasingly rocky landscape gave the strange sensation that they had traveled much further than a few minutes walk.

The life-giving sun hovered overhead in the clear blue sky, and small rocky peaks appeared on the horizon, growing larger as they approached the crest.

Then, after climbing for nearly an hour, they finally reached the hilltop. Eva and Amir marveled at the spectacular panoramic vista before them. The path went on for miles.

As far as the eye could see, a towering range of snow-capped mountains dominated the distant landscape. Waterfalls plunged from the rock, dropping hundreds of feet into large bodies of glistening blue-green water below. The two great rivers were nowhere to be seen, but this somehow slipped Eva's mind as she admired nature's fascinating beauty.

From where they stood atop the lofty foothills, all four seasons could be witnessed in a single view. They watched as strange new birds soared, apparently scanning the forest floors for food. Wild animals roamed freely in scattered fields far below, some stopping to sip from the edges of crystal clear streams.

Soft white clouds were strewn across the midday sky, not quite reaching the summits of the enormous rocky peaks. It was there, at the distant edge of the newfound paradise, that a single mountain towered over all the others. Amir and Eva were mesmerized by the beauty, and instantly humbled at the sight of their world's tallest peak.

CHAPTER
10

Amir and Eva admired the fascinating landscape for several minutes before deciding to continue along the path. As they began, they were startled by a powerful series of winds blowing up from the valley below. It chilled the two young travelers to the bone, and caused them to crouch next to a nearby tree for shelter. They shielded their faces from the wind so as not to get dust in their eyes.

After a few minutes, the blustery winds died down, becoming a gentle breeze once again. When the children stood and uncovered their eyes, they noticed a beautiful box sitting on the path, just a few meters ahead.

Upon hurrying to the chest, they observed its unique features. It was made of mahogany, and its sides were adorned with symbolic inscriptions. A solid gold lock appeared to secure its contents from uninvited looters. However, when Eva gave it a gentle pull...it opened with ease. They turned to look at one another; both equally anxious to discover what it contained.

Together, they opened the ancient box, and took accountability of the contents. To their surprise, the items inside were not old at all, but instead appeared postmodern. Inside the chest were two pairs of well-made leather hiking boots, two warm downy jackets, and two fleece winter hats. Trusting that the items were gifts from the mysterious old woman who had promised them "tools for the journey," they donned the gear and prepared to march on.

However, as Eva tested the pockets of her newfound coat, something else caught her attention. She paused, out of mere surprise, looking at Amir before removing the item from her jacket. He stared back in anticipation, having heard the rustling of the supplementary item. As Eva removed the item from her pocket, their eyes opened wide at the sight of the ancient rolled parchment. The scroll was sealed, and tied with durable red string.

Excited, they quickly unraveled the string that held the scroll in place. An eagle, with its wings spread wide, was embroidered on the golden seal. Amir took only a brief second to observe the seal before tearing it open and revealing the scroll's message.

Unable to read, Eva was pleased to see that the scroll contained pictures, and not a written message.

While the image on the scroll appeared to be a large circular map, it did not show any obvious sign of treasure. Instead, there was a beautifully painted landscape with an uncanny resemblance to the view from where they now stood.

From the bottom edge of the circle, a path wandered into the distance. It weaved through the foothills, went east up the alpine slopes, and disappeared just below the summit. The trail then re-emerged on the western face, and climaxed at the peak of the great mountain. A painted sun overhead illuminated the entire scene.

Along the path were three small, but identical symbols, each in the form of a featureless human being.

In a grid of miniature rectangles below the map, there was an assortment of colorful flags. While they did not count each of the flags, there appeared to be at least one hundred. All were unfamiliar to Eva, though Amir did recognize a few.

Unsure of what to make of the scroll, Amir rolled it up and handed it to Eva. She thanked him for his trust, and placed the scroll safely in her jacket pocket. After careful consideration, they decided not to abandon the fine chest. It was possibly a gift from the old woman, and therefore might be an integral part of their search for the treasure.

The ambitious young travelers took hold of the handles at opposite ends of the chest, lifted carefully with their legs, and started north for the soaring mountains up ahead.

It was the path to the secret treasure, which they would locate very soon. For The Great Mystery had assured them that the treasure was nearby, but difficult to find. Having considered her cryptic riddle, and studied the guidance of their scroll, they agreed that they were en route to the greatest mountain's summit. Certainly, there was nowhere more difficult to reach than there.

CHAPTER
11

It soon became clear that the cobblestone path would not lead them on an easy journey, but Amir and Eva were determined to find the secret treasure. Moving forward with heightened motivation, they made the gradual descent into the evergreen valley below. In the distance, the great mountain loomed.

Oddly, their muscles seemed to gain strength as they hiked, rather than becoming fatigued.

During conversation, Eva noticed obvious unintended fluctuations in Amir's voice. It was actually quite amusing, so she pretended not to notice. After a while, it went away, but his voice remained slightly deeper than before. Her friend had grown taller and more broad-shouldered as well.

While Amir failed to notice his changing characteristics, his mind was not eluded by Eva's own remarkably strange transformation. In addition to gaining a few inches in height, she had developed curves in her figure at the hips and chest.   He struggled not to stare, but found himself constantly tempted.   Soon, he became accustomed to the changes, and learned to respect her for the virtue that she possessed within.

Suddenly, he put his hand on her shoulder and stopped her from walking any further. Unable to contain his observations any longer, Amir finally spoke up.

"Eva," he said, "you've grown at least six inches, since we picked up this box on the ridge. Something weird is going on."

"Now that you say so, I think you're right," Eva replied. "I guess I was paying more attention to you than to myself.   It is strange, isn't it?"

"Strange?" Amir asked awkwardly, "It's incredible. We have only been moving for a short time, but you seem to have aged at least five years."

Eva considered the possibility. *We do seem to be aging rather quickly*, she thought.

"Perhaps it has something to do with this mysterious box," she suggested.   "Do you think the box is the treasure?"

"No way," Amir answered quickly. "I'm sure of it."

Eva was curious how he could be so sure. The box seemed to have given them power, as the old woman had said it would. Then again, she also said they would be given the tools for the journey.

"You've grown nearly a foot since leaving the ridge," she explained to Amir. "You have a bit of fuzz growing on your face too. Your shoulders and chest have broadened, and your voice has deepened quite a bit."

Eva paused as Amir felt the hair that had begun growing on his chin. "If you noticed that I was changing, why didn't you say anything sooner?" she asked.

"Look around," replied Amir. "Everything changes. There's nothing to worry about."

"Save me the 'follow the stream' speech this time," Eva said with frustration. "I know how the seasons change and all that. But we aren't like them. We shouldn't be aging this fast."

"We are part of nature just like everything else," he explained, to her initial disapproval. "Some things change slow, and others fast, but everything changes with time. Don't think of it as a bad thing. Maybe we're just aging in preparation for our positions as world leaders. Did you think of that? Nobody would ever permit us to unite the world as little kids."

She saw what he was getting at, and realized he was right.

"I'm sorry," she said. "Things haven't exactly been normal in the past day or so. Sorry if I'm a little short tempered. I don't know what has gotten into me lately."

"Just relax and enjoy the journey," Amir said as he attempted to calm Eva's unusual anxiety. "In case you've forgotten already, we're in this thing together."

Eva was feeling better about the changes. She allowed Amir to finish offering his wisdom with hopes that she could learn from his unique outlook on life.

"We can learn everything we need to know from nature," he said confidently. "If we pay attention in life, few things will come as a surprise. In fact, change alone, is what we can count on."

Eva smiled at the awkwardness of such words coming from a young teenager. "You learned all that from the trees?" she teased. "Unbelievable."

"Nature is more than just the trees. Our bodies, our ideas, our relationships... change is the pattern of our lives. Why act like it's a big deal?" Amir replied, apparently not getting the joke.

With both teens now confident that their rapid aging was part of the old woman's ongoing series of unwarranted gifts, they continued to advance along the path.

"Do you know what I see when I look at the trees?" asked Eva as they traveled happily toward the base of the great mountains.

"What's that?" Amir asked.

"Trees," Eva answered. "When I look at the trees... I see trees."

"Very funny," Amir said sarcastically.

"But to me, they are very beautiful trees," Eva continued. "I guess I just don't see past their beauty like you do. I notice their many types, sizes, textures, and colors. I've even thought about how they compliment the land, as if placed there by a great landscaper."

It was becoming clear to Amir that, even though he was wise, he could stand to learn a few things from Eva as well.

"I'm inspired by the trees, and the water too, for that matter. I just don't see life lessons when I look at them like you do."

Having realized that the peasant girl was much more intelligent than he had originally assumed, Amir responded.

"Well," he said, "I'm beginning to realize why we were chosen to find this treasure together."

CHAPTER
12

As Amir and Eva traversed the foothills and approached the great mountain, the sun began to set. With nowhere to stop for the evening, they faced another frightening night in the dark, this time much further from home. Having nothing but the scroll to guide them, they pulled it out and surveyed the map. With what was left of the daylight, they tried to pinpoint some trace of nearby civilization. Unfortunately, there was nothing of the sort.

Eva pointed out the three human symbols on the map, and noticed that one was near the base of the mountain. They waited for the old woman to appear and save them once again. Yet as the sun disappeared over the horizon, it seemed they would have no such luck.

Fearing another night in the cold shadowy woods, they hurried on ahead in search of shelter. Worst-case scenario, they would at least make their way closer to the summit; where they were sure to find the treasure. Just the possibility of ruling the world was enough to keep them excited while they walked. They moved onward throughout the night.

With endless energy flowing through their bodies, and a newfound sense of invincibility, Eva and Amir walked as fast as they could. While it presented little challenge, the weight of the wooden chest put a slight strain on their shoulders and hands as they lugged it along.

The darkness was thick in the absence of the moon. Nevertheless, Eva and Amir marched on with determination. Finally, the sun began to rise, and they waited anxiously to see how high they had climbed during the night. To their disappointment however, what they discovered left them both in shock. They could not understand what they saw.

"What's going on?" Eva turned to her friend and asked. "We walked all night as fast as we could, but it seems we haven't moved an inch."

"You've got me," replied Amir, equally confused. "It seems we would have been half-way up by now. This place looks just like where we were when the sun set last night."

In fact, it was.

They checked the path carefully to ensure they had not gone astray. As expected, the weathered stones remained perfectly arranged on the trail beneath their feet. They looked up at the mountain, confused. *Nothing about the journey has been normal thus far*, thought Amir. *Why would it change now?*

As Amir continued looking around in disbelief, Eva spotted smoke rising from somewhere up ahead. Excited at the possibility of making social contact, they hurried up the trail. After rounding the final corner, they were struck by the beauty of the architectural masterpiece that appeared before them. Built right into the base of the great mountain, the magnificent stone temple was like nothing they had ever seen.

They approached with caution, eager to learn more.

CHAPTER
13

The exquisite temple protruded from the mountainside, one-third hidden by the sheer granite cliffs. It had been constructed of large, clean-cut white stone, and its domed roof was a feat of engineering never before seen in their time. Flowering green vines crept from the ground up the enormous pillars, that were spaced evenly across the temple's curved face, where a spacious veranda wrapped around the front. From the center, a long staircase led to the ground below, becoming wider upon descent. Colossal oaks guarded the entryway, one on each side of the steps.

It was unlike any building Eva had ever seen, and she admired the detail and design of the great structure. Amir, on the other hand, had grown up in a royal palace, and the temple evoked memories of home. Each of them noted the lack of smoke anywhere in the area.

At the top of the staircase, a sophisticated looking, white-bearded man motioned with his hand for them to approach.

"Well, I guess we should go up there," Eva suggested.

"Yes," agreed Amir. "Maybe he can tell us how to find the treasure. If not, I'm sure he can offer some advice on how to navigate these mountains."

They approached the stairs of the great temple, exhausted from walking all night. Between them, they carried the fine wooden chest, still unsure of what it might be for. They began to climb, ascending nearly thirty steps before reaching the terrace. At the top, Amir and Eva stood face to face with the distinguished elder gentleman.

The old man exuded confidence without even speaking a word. His tan skin and fierce blue eyes complimented his thick white hair and beard. He wore only a toga, made of the finest linen in the world. On his feet, he wore brown leather sandals: a luxury that few in Eva's village could afford. He seemed unusually content, as if he sought nothing but the present moment. Then, after an awkward moment of silence, he spoke.

"Good morning," the old man said with enthusiasm. "I am Aristotle. I see that you have journeyed from afar, and have brought with you a fine wooden chest. How is it that I can serve you?"

The travelers were surprised to be offered service by a man of his apparent status. Such a thing was rare in their time.

"Well Sir," the boy began, "I'll do my best to explain." He took a deep breath before continuing with the story. "My name is Amir, and my friend is Eva." He placed his hand on Eva's shoulder as he introduced her. "We have come from a fertile land between the two great rivers. Eva is from the east, and I'm from the west. We were advised by a mysterious old woman to follow this path to a secret treasure."

"Ah," the old man replied, confirming his interest by putting his hand to his chin. "What sort of treasure?"

"One that would enable us to unite the entire world," Eva added with excitement. "All we have to guide us is this ancient scroll." She removed it from her jacket, unrolled it, and handed it to the old man.

"Well then," he said, surprised that they would hand over such a valuable piece to their puzzle. "I guess you're a trusting young lady." Eva dropped her head slightly with embarrassment, but maintained eye contact. "Lucky for you, I have seen the world, and have no desire to obtain that kind of power." Eva felt relieved. "In the future however, I would hesitate before revealing your objectives to strangers."

Understanding his point, she nodded in approval.

"Perhaps you are the chosen ones of the ancient myth," the old man explained. "There are others out here in the wilderness... others with questionable intent. They all seek the treasure, but none have held the scroll."

Eva now realized that their scroll was indeed a treasure map. Her face lit up with excitement as the old man continued.

"People come from all around to climb the great mountain, but few, if any, have ever reached the summit. In time, the path leads to burnt or broken bridges, and they can no longer journey forward to the top." The old man paused for a moment to allow his words to sink in. "At least, that's what I've heard."

Sensing that Aristotle was sincere, Amir offered an apology. "We will heed your advice, and be more careful in the future." He bowed slightly, signifying respect, before asking an important question.

"Why did you build your temple at the base of this great mountain? You seem to have the tools for the ascent. Don't you at least want to know what's up there?"

Understanding the curiosity of young teens, the philosopher knew he could not deter them from their journey. Nor did he feel it necessary to try. He thought to himself, *"All follow one path or another, and must experience life in their own unique way."*

"Oh Amir," said the old man while placing a hand on each of their shoulders, "I think it's time that you and Eva come inside and meet my family."

CHAPTER
14

As the great teacher spoke, Amir listened intently. Eva, however, had dazed off into a world of her own. She was awestruck by the amazing temple, and its dreamlike setting. Spring was in the air, and the birds were singing their songs once again.

Aristotle stepped aside and raised his hand, motioning for them to enter. Amir tapped Eva on the shoulder to get her attention.

"Hey," he whispered, "let's go."

She followed him into the majestic structure, never quite taking her mind off of everything else. The sage followed behind as they entered through a giant archway, which led to the rotunda.

Each footstep echoed throughout the room as they entered the massive sanctuary. The colossal exterior pillars stood like guards against the invading rays of sunlight, permitting some to enter, but denying others. The light resembled a midday break in an otherwise dark tropical storm. Above, the towering dome displayed vibrant paintings of angels, soaring amid stunning scenic worlds. At the dome's highest point was a vivid stained-glass window. Its transparent, multi-color image was brilliant; a thin yellow band around a dark-blue center. Random specs of white glass gave the appearance of stars in the night sky, eclipsing the golden sun.

A large circular meeting table sat directly beneath the lower circumference of the dome high above. It was made of dark, polished wood, resembling that of the fine chest. Its center had been neatly removed, allowing the light from above to shine down on the marble floor within.

Prominent icons of the spiritual path sat quietly around the outer edge of the table. Each with a leather-bound book placed neatly in front of them. The books would remain closed for the duration of the meeting. Then, like pillars of faith, they stood in unison as Amir and Eva entered the room. Aristotle followed closely behind.

As the three of them arrived at the large desk, Eva and Amir noticed only one vacant seat. The sage did not pause as he calmly took his place, leaving his guests with nowhere to go. The teens exchanged uncomfortable looks, momentarily unsure of what to do next.

After a brief hesitation, Aristotle politely suggested that they stand in the center, where all could see. The wise philosopher used only his hand in motioning to a narrow opening in the table where they could enter. The teens understood, and followed his guidance. The missing section of table was conveniently located for such an occasion.

Amir and Eva could feel the probing stares of the mysterious family, piercing through them like arrows as they stood on the target. On center stage, the teens were surrounded.

Aristotle introduced his guests to the family as they listened in silence. He explained the purpose of their visit, as described on the terrace outside. Following the introductions, the sage took his seat. Once seated comfortably, the others followed him almost instantly. Sliding chairs screeched briefly on the marble floor as the family settled in for what appeared to be an interview.

All the while, Amir and Eva remained standing in the center of the massive domed temple, surrounded by inquisitive looks.

"This is my family," Aristotle began. He motioned with his hands at the people surrounding the table. "As you can see; we appear very different, but are related by our state of mind. We come from different nations, not different worlds. From diverse paths, we have arrived at this great temple... now members of this sacred family."

Amir and Eva stood by, silently scanning the family as they listened.

"Many years pass by between visitors around here," the elder explained. "One by one, they come and go, unable to find what they think they need. Every now and then however, someone arrives, understanding the true nature of existence. They have seen the mountaintop, and no longer desire possession of the elusive 'secret treasure'. In a sense, their search is over. When these people arrive at the temple, we welcome them into our family."

Eva and Amir began to feel more at ease after realizing the good nature of the man's family. They took note of the family's diverse array of clothing, facial features, and skin complexions.

"I see that you carry an empty box," Aristotle continued. "Might I ask why?"

"The box was a gift," explained Eva. "It contained tools needed for our journey. We are carrying it in case it is needed on our journey."

Unsure of why anyone would drag along additional baggage for such an arduous trek, the old man shrugged his shoulders, and pretended to be satisfied with the answer.

"Perhaps it can be used here," he explained. "My family and I have something vital to share with you. Our gift will ensure your successful ascent of the great mountain."

The curious teens focused their full attention on the old man, suddenly eager to hear more.

"I will give you a choice, and the two of you will decide. One way or another, you will leave here with what you need. For we have been advised of your status, and directed to assist you with your quest."

Amir and Eva looked at each other in astonishment, wondering how they knew so much. "Don't get too excited," Aristotle added. "We can only help you so much."

"I'm afraid I don't understand," said Amir in frustration. "If we deserve this treasure so much, why not just give it to us now so we can use it?"

"The answer is simple," replied the sage. "One must first climb the mountain, if they wish to see the view."

CHAPTER
15

With their backs to one another, Eva and Amir slowly spun clockwise in the center of the table. The saints in the room possessed many priceless books, and were prepared to offer them as a gift. Their books were like treasure maps, much like the scroll that Amir and Eva now possessed.

After allowing the silence in the room to become a bit tense, Aristotle made his offer.

"You may have your clue in one of two forms," he explained. "Each of these books contains stories, lessons, and most of all... wisdom. Each can serve as your guide while you search this land for the secret treasure. Having such books might be a great advantage at some stage of your odyssey." He paused to let them consider the positives before going on to the next point. "On the other hand, the stories in our books vary on the surface. Each is written in language that you most likely will not understand."

Having originally thought the books to be a very useful tool, Amir and Eva now considered the issue at hand. Without the proper literacy, the books might cause more harm than good.

"If you desire," he continued, "you may have these books to use as your guide. Perhaps the two of you can learn to decipher the language with which they were written, and they may be of great use. Nonetheless, they are very heavy, and will bring added fatigue during transport."

He paused to let the first option sink in, and then continued with the second.

"If you desire to move *quickly*," he offered with inflection in his voice, "I can save you time and effort by offering a bit of insight."

The overwhelmed teens in the center of the room welcomed the idea of saving time.

"What is this insight you speak of?" inquired Amir.

"The wisdom of our library exists within the nature of life itself." Eva looked skeptical, knowing that only Amir would see things that way.

"But what makes the books so hard to understand?" she asked.

Aristotle explained, "If a student wishes to understand a word; that is easy. However, if her desire is to understand a masterpiece, she must have patience. The student must learn to see the final product through the eyes of its inventor. Otherwise, how will one appreciate the difference between an apprentice and the master?"

Eva could see his point, but remained silent, absorbing the knowledge of the great teacher.

"A sacred book is the author's artistic masterpiece," Aristotle confirmed. "It is the translation of nature into words, using imagery. Our books are written in a universal language. Their truth lies not in their historical accuracy, but in the impressions they leave on one's soul. In this way, we have protected our message from translation and deceit, so that only the worthy will understand. For this reason, you may find them quite confusing."

Amir got his point, knowing that they most likely would not find use of the great books without the time to study. They needed to travel, not read.

"Whether you accept the books, or look to nature for guidance, you will find the same truth." He allowed them a moment to consider the offer. "When you realize the true nature of life, it will guide you to your treasure...and the power you seek."

"What if we make it up the mountain and can't find the treasure?" asked Eva. "I don't want to have to come back for the books, when we can just bring them now."

"I understand," replied Aristotle, "that you cannot go home until you find the treasure. Just be careful. Haste alone should not persuade you to abandon the guidance of wise people. If you cannot trust a sage, who can you trust?"

Eva agreed, but also realized that the mahogany chest would be a perfect means by which to transport the sacred books. *What else would it be used for?* She wondered.

It was clear to Aristotle that he had not yet gained their trust. "You can either trust me, or bring the books along. Either way, you will have what you need when you leave."

Eva was excited to get her hands on the books. She wanted desperately to unlock their mysteries and find the secret treasure.

Amir, on the other hand, was confident in his ability to understand nature's mysterious language. He was wise enough to know that carrying the books would add a tremendous burden to their trip. Nevertheless, it was a similar book that had helped his family acquire their kingdom. *If one book united my own kingdom*, he thought, *surely we might need many books to unite the world.*

"Well, what is your decision?" Aristotle asked.

Eva and Amir did not yet have the faith to go blindly up the mountain. Nor did they feel they should. They needed to read the books in order to put the pieces together for themselves.

"Well Sir," Amir began, "we appreciate your advice, but have chosen to accept the books."

"As you wish," said the philosopher.

One by one, the spiritual leaders stood, offered their books to the young couple, and exited the sanctuary. Each book fit neatly into the mahogany chest like a puzzle, filling it to the brim with sacred knowledge. When they had finished, Amir and Eva closed the lid tightly, and lifted the box.

Much to their surprise, it was even heavier than they had imagined.

CHAPTER
16

Amir and Eva carried the heavy wooden chest as they walked out onto the terrace with Aristotle. While exiting through the giant pillars, they observed the wooded land from which they had traveled the previous day. The view was spectacular, and offered a much different perspective than before.

Scattered across the distant forest through which the cobblestone path had led, smoke escaped the chimneys of hundreds of tiny buildings. Many of the structures appeared to be just a short distance from the path.

"What are those places?" Eva asked.

"Oh yes, the inns around here are spectacular," replied Aristotle. "Each has a nice place to rest and enjoy the evening. Many of them even offer complimentary meals for guests. I'm surprised you didn't stop at one last night."

"They weren't there last night," answered Eva, feeling a bit confused. "We searched for a place for hours, but when we didn't find one, we just kept walking."

"Ah," the old man sighed, "but you did not save a minute by walking through the night." He raised his right hand, and pointed to a place in the distant landscape. Sure enough, they could see the great rivers sparkling to the east and west. Their villages sat peacefully on the shores, still within view. They couldn't have been more than ten miles from home. "The inns have been there all along," he said. Amir and Eva looked out again, unsure of how they could have missed so much.

As their time together drew to an end, Aristotle offered his parting words, "As I said inside the temple, there is wisdom all around." He raised his arms to the world around, and then lowered only the left. Pointing outward in the direction of the smoking chimneys, he gave them one final clue; "You will find your secret treasure...by learning from the inns."

Suddenly, the gentle breeze accelerated, and began to stir wildly around the temple. Dust filled the morning air, negatively affecting their visibility. Hurricane-force winds howled down from the massive slopes of the great mountain, causing them to cover their eyes and crouch onto the temple veranda. As the frightened teens cowered on the floor, the old man stood tall in the cloudless storm, apparently unaffected by the surrounding chaos. Then, in a newfound booming voice, he warned them of the hazards to come.

"Guard the books with your life!" he warned in a thunderous voice. "Do not let them out of your sight!" Despite the howling winds, every word was clearly audible. "Without wisdom, their power will destroy your future kingdom."

Amir and Eva had heard every word. It was a warning of the utmost importance.

Shortly thereafter, the blustery winds died down, and peace returned to the mountainside. The dust fell from the air, scattering among the land, and finally settled upon the earth once again. The teens regrouped, dusted off their clothes, and wiped sand from their burning eyes. Though they remained crouched on the ground, they were no longer on the terrace.

Beneath their feet, was the well-built cobblestone path. The glorious temple had vanished into thin air... and the wise philosopher was nowhere to be seen.

CHAPTER
17

Amir and Eva were stunned. Neither had considered the frightening paradox of possessing such great power. Either way, it was too late now. The only way to protect the sacred books was to bring them along.

They shook off their momentary disappointment and regrouped their thoughts. With the temple now gone, they stood alone at the foot of the great mountain. Their new baggage was heavy, but the chest full of books was their new responsibility. If they wished to inherit a kingdom worth ruling, they would have to carry the weight. *Better a little work now than a future of regret later*, they thought.

Each grabbed hold of a handle, and lifted the heavy box from the ground. They felt the strain in their shoulders immediately, but moved on regardless, in search of their treasure.

As they entered the domain of the legendary mountains, the incline of the trail increased sharply. The stone path hugged the edge of the towering cliffs, often switching back to lessen the vertical strain. The view from the walkway was spectacular. Far below, their path meandered like a snake through the trees, finally disappearing beyond the distant hills. With every step, their world seemed to include more and more. Their perspective was slowly transforming.

Though the changing path made them curious, there was only one to follow. Eva thought often about Amir's quote from the previous day, *"Everything changes,"* he had said. *The Scroll depicted only one way up the mountain, and this has to be it.*

As they rounded the mountainside, Eva considered the old man's final clue. "What can the inns teach us about treasure?" Eva asked Amir. "Got any ideas?"

"Well," Amir explained, "if we would have slowed down and paid attention, we would have seen the inns. In our haste, we arrived at the temple with tired minds, and made a poor decision about these books."

Eva contemplated his rational, and understood the lesson.

"I guess that was the old man's way of saying I told you so," she added.

"Yes, I think you're right," said Amir with a chuckle. "Who says philosophers have no sense of humor?"

Although they both agreed that bringing the books was probably not the easiest way to go, they were glad to have them. If they ran into trouble finding the treasure, they could always search through the books for assistance. In addition, there didn't seem to be anyone else around to cause them trouble.

Perhaps it will just take a few extra days to find the treasure, Eva thought. *Better late than never.* The additional effort would be well worth the splendid prize at the end.

CHAPTER
18

An hour or so passed as they trekked up the path. The heavy wooden chest full of books was really taking its toll on their bodies. Despite their youth, they struggled with the load, and required frequent breaks to recuperate.

As they made their way around a large rocky outcrop, Eva noticed something obstructing the path about one hundred meters ahead.

"Look!" she exclaimed as she pointed to the trail up ahead.

Amir suddenly noticed the object as well.

Unsure of what it was, but eager to find out, they picked up their pace, hurrying to get a closer look. As they approached the object, they noticed that it was a wheeled device, likely used for transport.

The device was made of fine wood, and resembled the chest in its peculiar detail and spectacular design. It had two extended handles on one end, apparently for the operators to push with. Eva admired the brilliant craftsmanship, as well as the inventor. With the flawed perception that everything existed for them alone, they instantly decided how it could be of use.

They carefully loaded the chest onto the wagon, grabbed hold of the handles, and began to push the wheeled vehicle up the hill. Immediately, they felt they had made a good choice. Though they moved at about the same pace, they needed fewer breaks. Their legs bore most of the tension now, and their shoulders began a much-needed recovery. It seemed there would be no easy way to make the trip, only varying levels of difficulty.

Amir and Eva pushed into the ground with their feet and leaned forward, slowly but surely making their way up the mountain. They paused to regain their strength now and then, and to take in the breath-taking views.

Their age continued to accelerate with every difficult step up the steep incline. The sun slowly fell from the sky, hinting that nightfall would soon arrive. Having learned from the past, Eva hinted that they should begin looking carefully for a place to settle in for the night. Amir agreed, not wanting to make the same mistake again.

In spite of the lesson learned earlier at the temple, this situation was different. Rather than walking quickly through a forest filled with inns, they now wandered on a steep rocky mountainside, far from civilization. At the pace they had been moving with their wagon full of books, passing an inn without noticing would have been nearly impossible.

Their hopes of finding an inn began to dwindle as the setting sun painted a magnificent pink and orange sky. Other than a few patches of brown grass, the rocky environment was much too high for the growth of most plants, ensuring the visibility of anything nearby. At first look, there was nothing. Then, as they approached a curve in the path ahead, they were welcomed by an unexpected surprise.

A multi-room inn sat stilted on the side of the mountain, serving as a stopping point for travelers on their way to the summit. The single-story building was made of stones, which appeared to have been cut from the mountain itself. Thick wooden shingles protected the roof, and two small windows revealed the light from inside. Facing the surrounding vista out back was a large observation deck, complete with two tables and matching chairs.

As they neared the resting point, another fascinating discovery awaited them. Just past the inn, the path ended abruptly at the edge of a sheer cliff. An old wooden bridge connected the path to its reemergence on the other side. Below the bridge, a bottomless gorge dropped thousands of feet into a dark river far below. Fortunately, the bridge seemed just wide enough for their cart to pass through.

After a bit of rest, it was sure to be an exciting day ahead.

CHAPTER
19

More than half way up the mountain, and with the sun setting fast, they could not have arrived at a better time. Deciding to rest up and cross the gorge in the morning, Eva and Amir pushed their wheeled cart full of books to the main entry of the quaint, but cozy mountainside cottage. The door was conveniently propped open from the inside.

As they approached, the most beautiful woman they had ever seen stepped outside to welcome them. Her skin was fair and smooth, highlighted by her bright green eyes, straight dark hair, and remarkable smile. She wore a thin black knee-length dress, accentuating the gentle curves of her perfect figure. When she spoke, her enchanting voice nearly hypnotized the tired young adults.

"Welcome," she said, being sure to make eye contact with each of them. "How may I help you?"

"We would like a room for the night," replied Amir. "We have traveled all day, and would prefer to rest until morning."

"Where are you headed?" she curiously asked. "There's not much up here you know."

"Tomorrow we hope to reach the summit," answered Amir without hesitation.

"The summit is a long way up," said the woman. "I have never known anyone to make it that far. It can get pretty treacherous with the ice and snow."

"So we've been told," said Amir. "We'll be fine. We just need some rest before we continue."

Concerned about revealing their intentions, they made sure not to mention the scroll, or the valuable contents of their cart.

"Very well then," the woman said, having warned them of the mountain's dangerous past. She invited them into the inn to show them a room, but Amir did not want to leave the cart unsupervised.

"Are there currently any other visitors?" Amir asked. "I'd rather not leave our cart unsecured throughout the night. Maybe we should bring the items inside."

"I fully understand your concern," she replied. "At this time, the inn is vacant. We don't normally get much traffic up here. I'm actually quite surprised to see the two of you this evening. Normally, we get advanced notice from climbers."

"Well, we were just following our map," replied Amir. He immediately noticed his mistake as he felt Eva's elbow in his ribs. They glanced briefly at one another, and then smiled awkwardly at the innkeeper. He was sure he had messed up, but the woman seemed to pay no mind to his slip of the tongue. They settled back down, glad to have avoided potential disaster.

"If you would like," the woman continued, "I can put you in the room with a window to the road. You can park your cart right outside, and leave your window open. If anyone should mess with it, which I do not foresee, you will surely have time to intervene."

They considered the arrangements, and without much else to choose from, they agreed.

"I'll be here all night as well," she added. "If I hear or see anyone, I'll alert you immediately." She ended with a reassuring smile.

"Sounds good to me," said Amir. Eva nodded in agreement. They had seen no one all day, and did not plan to sleep for long. Certainly, by sunrise they would be up and ready to go again.

The gorgeous young woman invited them in, holding the door as they entered. As Eva passed through the entryway, she noticed a strangely familiar design on the upper part of the door. The woman's head obstructed most of the yellow and blue stained glass viewing window as they entered, but it caught Eva's eye nonetheless. An eerie feeling crept through her tired body as they made their way inside. She was unable to identify the source of her anxiety, so she decided to keep the information to herself.

The woman showed them to their room, opened their window, and wished them good night. Amir was pleased to see the cart full of books sitting just outside. *We couldn't have stumbled upon a more perfect place to relax*, he thought to himself before taking a visual survey of the room.

The accommodations were simple, but pleasant. A small table and two wooden chairs sat neatly in the left corner, and a full-size bed extended from the center of the far wall. Except for two bronze candleholders, the walls were free of decorations. Short reddish candles glowed quietly on each sconce as they burned.

Eva was intrigued by a small box on the table, and decided to pick it up. While examining its contents, she found four tiny wooden sticks with charcoal colored tips.

Unsure of what they were, she took one out for more careful observation.

"Do you have any idea what these are?" she asked Amir.

"Never seen anything like it," he replied. "Hold on a second."

He opened the door and saw the beautiful woman standing in the hall, apparently watching for visitors, as promised.

"Excuse me," he said. "I'm sorry to bother you already, but what exactly are these for?" He held out the box for her to see.

"Oh my," she replied with a gentle laugh. "Where have you two been lately? Those are matches. They've really revolutionized the night life around here."

Amir did not catch the sarcasm.

She struck one against the side of the box as a demonstration, and it instantly caught fire. After allowing the travelers to observe attentively, she extinguished the flame and then flicked the useless fuse out of the door onto the stony path.

"Wow," Eva said, "that was amazing! It seems so effortless."

"They are convenient," said the beautiful woman. "But use them cautiously. These are the last three at the inn. We should be getting more any day now, but resupply is unpredictable around here. There are just too many variables."

She handed them back to Amir, and he placed them safely into his pocket with the scroll.

"Is there anything else I can help you with?" she asked.

"No thanks," Amir replied. "We really appreciate your help."

"I do what I can," said the woman with a friendly smile. Her dazzling green eyes still glowed in the dim light of the hall.

Upon exchanging a cheerful farewell, Amir and Eva returned to their room, closing the door behind them.

Worn out from the day's exertion, they removed their coats and shoes before lying side-by-side on the comfy bed. Shadows danced on the ceiling above as they stared. They reminisced about their incredible experience at the temple, and shared their surprise about finding the inn. Each silently considered the treasure hidden somewhere nearby, and how it could possibly offer such extraordinary influence.

The flicker of the candles in the dark room caused their eyelids to become surprisingly heavy. Gravity pulled them softly downward as their heads sunk tranquilly into their downy pillows. They imagined themselves to be alone on the great mountain, thereby never suspecting the true magnitude of their circumstances. Their conscious thoughts dissolved into dreams as they faded into a deep slumber.

CHAPTER
20

A deafening cry went out in the midst of the night. The frightening sound echoed off of the mountain's towering granite walls. Amir and Eva jumped out of bed, awakened instantly by the scare. Their warm breath turned to mist each time they exhaled, highlighting the chill in the sinister alpine atmosphere.

"What on earth was that?" asked Amir.

"You heard it too?" Eva asked, now realizing that it wasn't just a bad dream.

Unsure of what had happened, but eager to investigate, they searched for a way to light the bedside candles, which had apparently burned out as they slept. Eva stumbled and fell to the ground while trying to find the door in the dark. Amir hurried over to help, and offered his hand in assistance. Much to his surprise, she did not respond. The terrifying look in her eyes sent chills down his spine, as she looked right past him, and up toward the ceiling.

"Look," Eva whispered, barely able to speak. She pointed, instead of taking his hand, momentarily disoriented from the shock of what she saw.

As Amir slowly lifted his gaze skyward, his stomach turned. Still unaware of what had happened, an onslaught of guilt crushed them like nothing they had ever known.

In place of the ceiling that he expected to see, stars dotted the otherwise black midnight sky. A foggy haze surrounded the inn, made worse by the ominous scent of smoke. A burnt out wooden frame was all that remained. Only then did Eva notice the ashes on her hands and knees from where she had stumbled.

Little by little, their eyes adjusted to the dim light of the starlit sky. Turning their attention through the missing exterior wall, they looked down to the valley far below. They instantly understood the bizarre, smoke-filled heavens above.

As far as their eyes could see, flames engulfed the landscape. Everything in view was ablaze. The reflections on the rivers and lakes made them appear to be burning as well. All around, chilling screams filled the air. In spite of the fires, an icy wind blew through the shell of what used to be the inn. Eva and Amir shivered in the cold, unable to speak.

Though it did not occur to them immediately, concern for the books suddenly hit them like a bolt of lightning. With no need to go to the window, Amir and Eva carefully exited the inn through what was left of the wall.

On the path outside, their fine wooden cart remained, somehow unharmed by the catastrophe. Nonetheless, their jaws dropped in dismay as they realized what they had done.

The sacred books were gone, and their future kingdom lay in ruins.

CHAPTER
21

The sun failed to rise that morning, and the icy cold breeze did not let up. Amir and Eva sat shivering on the side of the cliff with their legs dangling into the bottomless gorge. As the shrill screams reverberated in the canyon, they gradually became immune to the sound. They would be lucky to survive.

Their unfortunate circumstance was made worse by the missing bridge. The steep cliffs of the gorge were now connected by nothing but empty darkness, and the path could hardly be seen on the other side.

Their current situation clouded their vision of the future, much like the heavy smoke was erasing the stars in the sky. Their plans were burning even faster than the forest below.

Then out of nowhere, they began to hear the unmistakable grumble of stampeding cattle running furiously toward the gorge. The ground shook as their dark world closed

in.   Amir and Eva climbed to their feet,
unsure of what was going on.

Just then, seven warhorses appeared in
the distance, racing up the path from below.
With nowhere to go, the young couple felt
their lives coming to an end. Surely, a fall
into the cavernous gorge would kill them
long before they reached the bottom. They
waited patiently on death from the ledge as
the galloping horses drew near.

The oncoming cavalry of courageous,
battle hardened warriors approached the
gorge at full speed.   Then, as if suddenly
realizing the bridge was gone, they slid to a
sudden halt at the cliff's edge, nearly pushing
the frightened travelers to their deaths.

Realizing the end had not yet arrived,
Amir and Eva opened their eyes. The smoke
had cleared in the immediate vicinity, and
they could see clearly for the first time since
waking up.   The luminous moon hovered
overhead, somehow melting away the haze
between itself and the tense encounter on
the path down below.

Across the broad gorge, a mysterious
sentry observed the situation from afar. The
patrol consisted of three additional horses;
one black, one brown, and one white. Other
than their color, few details were visible
from such a distance. The strangest part was

not how they came from above, but that the three horses had only one rider.

Having approached from below, the other seven horsemen created an intimidating semi-circle near the ledge, giving Amir and Eva no chance of escape.

With three riders to his left, and three to his right, Alexander the Great sat atop his frighteningly strong black stallion. His armor shimmered in the moonlight as Bucephalas raised its front legs high off the ground, jolting The Great King only slightly. After letting out an intimidating wild neigh, the horse came crashing back to the earth, causing the ground to tremble once again.

Amir and Eva waited anxiously for the king to speak, unsure of where they had gone so terribly wrong.

CHAPTER
22

At only thirty years old, Alexander was about the same age as his newfound captives, yet he had already become the most powerful man in the world. The Great King removed his helmet, revealing his flowing black hair, and addressed the travelers in a commanding voice...as if the two, were one.

"I am Alexander of Macedon," he said with authority. "Who are you, and what are you doing on the great mountain?"

Amir and Eva had never heard of the king before. Nonetheless, he clearly controlled their destiny. Seeing that Amir was too frightened to speak, Eva decided to answer the king's questions.

"My name is Eva, and this is Amir," she said. "We have traveled from afar in an attempt to climb this great mountain. Amir is from the West, and I am from the East. Last night, we stayed here at the inn, and were planning to move on when daylight returned."

Surprised at how Eva had referred to the burnt-out building beside the cliff as an inn, The Great King suddenly became suspicious.

"I have ruled this land for many years," he said, looking into their eyes for the truth. "You must know the history of this place as well as anyone. It's been centuries since this inn was last occupied by guests." Amir and Eva wanted to speak up, but feared that a single word, whatever it was, would be their last. "Be careful with your story," he warned. "It's a long fall to the bottom of the gorge."

Having fully understood The Great King's warning, the troubled guests were unsure how to explain. Clearly there had been a serious misunderstanding. *There's no way we just slept for hundreds of years,* Eva thought to herself, though the scorched landscape below told a different story.

Not wanting to test Alexander's patience, she searched for answers.

"Why is the land on fire?" she asked, trying to change the subject.

He paused before answering, ready to crush them at the first hint of dishonesty. To his astonishment, the look in her eyes showed she was being sincere. He could not comprehend how they did not know.

"As the legend is told," he began, "a band of nomads wandered up this very path long ago... in search of a priceless hidden treasure."

CHAPTER
23

Knowing that any sudden movement could make them appear suspicious, Eva and Amir fought the urge to grab hands. They could see where this was going.

Alexander told the legend, much as it had been told throughout the ages.

"The nomads arrived at the canyon shortly after nightfall, and decided to spend a night at the inn before continuing on the next day. When they requested a room from the innkeeper, they were informed that there was no vacancy. Having traveled all day up the steep mountain, they were deeply discouraged, and decided to set up their tents on the path outside."

Amir and Eva listened attentively as they put the pieces together in their minds.

"As they began to unpack their tents," he continued, "they noticed that wheeled transport cart sitting outside the inn." Alexander pointed to the wooden cart by the inn, apparently not realizing the connection.

Amir and Eva tried to hide their remorse as the story went on.

"It is said," the king explained, "that a fine mahogany chest was carelessly hidden inside the cart. The nomads opened the chest and discovered it to be filled with ancient books. After browsing for only a few minutes, they realized how lucky they were. Mistaking the books for the secret treasure, they quietly removed the chest and returned to their village.

"The following day, they set up shop at the marketplace, and sold the books to travelers for a considerable profit. With their newfound wealth, the nomads rapidly gained power. They ruled without mercy for many years, causing their own desperate subjects to rise up, and revolt."

Finally, Eva spoke up, "So, is that what caused all this suffering?"

"That was only the beginning," Alexander responded.

She could not believe there was more. It seemed enough that they had lost the books and caused the destruction of the world. Nevertheless, The Great King continued to explain.

"In order to maintain their power, these ruthless leaders enforced harsh taxation, and even slavery, on those who already had nothing to give. With their additional wealth, they offered nothing to the people, but stored up fortunes for themselves."

Tears welled up in Eva's eyes as she realized the extent of the damage. At that moment, ruling the world had lost its appeal. Leaders everywhere were no longer envied, but despised.

"The power of the former nomads appeared unstoppable for many years, and it was thought by most that they ruled the entire world. But to their demise, they were heavily outnumbered, and the oppressed were eventually able to organize a successful uprising. This brought on a series of civil wars, and was followed by severe famine. In the wake of their weakened state, invaders from the north, south, east, and west, attacked them with merciless vengeance until the entire kingdom had been destroyed. Before long, their empire had dwindled into ruins, and the rulers became nomads... once again.

"In an ironic twist, the flags of the conquering nations bore familiar symbols, each representative of the stolen sacred books. As the legend explains, not one of the invading nations existed when the nomads first took power.

"As for the new rulers, they tried desperately to restore justice and peace to the land, but their attempts were short lived.

Without a common purpose to unite the people, they too eventually collapsed. Many great wars ensued, further destroying not only the landscape, but the trust which once existed in the world."

Amir and Eva only listened, hoping for any hint of a resolution.

"During their reign of power, the nomads believed it was the sacred books which had brought them sovereign authority over the world. They had no doubt that the books were the secret treasure. However, the ensuing destruction of their empire proved this to be false. For the legend states that when the real treasure is discovered, the world will become one.

"The nomads, having been attacked from every direction, realized that the world was much bigger than their kingdom. They had made a grave mistake here at the inn.

"Having realized this, the nomads returned to the great mountain, but to their disappointment, the bridge was gone. They looked out at the landscape and realized the destruction their evil empire had caused. From the second they had found the books, the nomads had considered themselves better than others. Because of this misconception, they lost everything.

"The wheeled cart has been here ever since, serving as a constant reminder that the real treasure still exists. Others have searched every inch of the path up to this point, but no treasure has been found. If it does exist, it is higher on the mountain.

"So, who are your friends?" Eva asked.

"We are The Council of War and Peace," Alexander explained, raising his arms to include those around him. "As such, we must ensure that the treasure is found.

"While even the power of a king is limited, the power of mankind is great. We have made our mark on the world, but are unable to advance beyond the gorge," he paused, and stared into their eyes before continuing. "Perhaps it is you who will journey on, find the secret treasure, and unite the world."

Amir and Eva suddenly felt as if the horsemen might not push them off the cliff after all. For what it seemed, the kings were just like the spiritual leaders at the temple. *Within a few minutes*, they thought, *these warriors will vanish, and the land will be restored to its original beauty.*

"How will anyone cross this gorge?" asked Amir. "It's too wide, and far too deep."

"Everything changes, isn't that right?" replied Alexander. "What you cannot imagine, does not change what is possible. Our world has many citizens. What was impossible for your ancestors is now possible for you. You must set the foundation, for the possibilities of tomorrow. I'm surprised that a man in your position has not figured that out."

"What do you mean, a man in my position?" asked Amir.

"You know what I mean," replied Alexander, thrusting his sword into the night sky.

With this, Amir and Eva knew their encounter with The Great King was over. It was perfect. They understood now. They had learned a valuable lesson. *Don't lose the books*, they thought. *Don't go to sleep and let people steal your things. Be more responsible.*

Much to their disappointment, however, the council did not vanish as predicted. The bridge did not magically reappear. The fires did not burn out, and the sun did not rise.

CHAPTER
24

Amir and Eva felt their hearts sink. Perhaps they would not get bailed out this time after all. Maybe they had failed at the bridge like the others, and The Great Mystery had chosen someone else more responsible for the job. They stared out into the burning night, imagining their dark futures before turning back to the horsemen.

"I'm terribly sorry to disappoint you Sir," said Amir, "but I don't think we're the ones for the job. We're clearly not qualified to unite the world. I'm sure of it."

Alexander corrected Amir for his mistake. "Perhaps you cannot put out the fires that consume the world as we speak, or build a bridge across this gorge. However, I assure you that more difficult things have been accomplished. The fatal end of every quest to unite the world has ended in the same way. Thankfulness turns to conceit, and we falsely believe that we are good enough alone."

Once again, Alexander raised his sword into the air as his courageous horse rose up on his back legs. The two seemed to be of the same mind; each one fueled by the other.

Just then, the night was awakened by a tremendous applause. Incredible cheers filled the night from behind The Great King, causing the mountain to vibrate beneath their feet. Thousands of people had gathered behind the horsemen, each packed in tight on the trail. The enormous military-style formation continued for miles into the darkness.

Bucephalas came crashing down once again.

"The impossible soon becomes possible when you change your perspective," said the wise king. "Is it not a miracle that you even exist? Then why not believe in yourself? Uniting the world effectively may require teamwork and shared purpose, but not miracles.

"Look within yourselves, and you will find the secret treasure. As I'm sure you've heard, it is near, but very hard to find. How will the people believe in you, if you do not believe in yourselves?"

Alexander smiled for the first time, noticing a newfound confidence in the eyes of the chosen ones.

"Many have gathered here today in support of your mission. These people hope to provide great assistance to the two of you. They have seen too much tyranny and injustice during their lifetimes, and have done their best to set things right. With your approval, they will rebuild the missing bridge."

Amir and Eva were instantly humbled by the generosity of the crowd.

Eva then asked the king one final question. "What have we done to deserve this? We have failed at simple things. What makes you think we will make it to the top of the mountain, or find the treasure that will unite the world?"

Alexander spoke for the crowd. "What has any of us done prior to our birth, which has made us deserving of the gift of life? Yet we are granted the gift, nonetheless. One must consider their motive when questioning why things happen as they do. Either observe and be thankful, or do something to help.

"Our mission in life is to learn, and opportunity exists in every moment. *What* we must learn is the ultimate question, and the secret treasure will contain the answer. Once you present the treasure to others, they will surely unite, for it will serve as the common purpose by which all can relate.

Eva and Amir had no idea what that purpose might be, but grew confident that they would know soon enough. In the meantime, there still existed a big problem...the bottomless gorge...without a bridge.

CHAPTER
25

This gorge represents a great void of understanding," Alexander began, "and it is here that you must learn another valuable lesson. The people who stand with me today have sacrificed their time, the most precious of all currency."

Eva and Amir bowed their heads in gratitude.

"As you walk across this canyon on our bridge, you must remember that one's post is not attained by merit alone, but by those who went before you... and paved the way."

Amir and Eva would probably never repay the men and women for what they were about to do, but it didn't matter. They thanked them all out loud, and then the show began.

Row by row, the people came forward, each carrying a single item. Some carried large stones, while others carried wood, and still others brought nails or other tiny, but equally significant items.

As each person went by, they added their element to the bridge, and then leapt miraculously into the night sky. They streaked like lasers into the heavens above, and as each one vanished, a new star appeared.

As the bridge made its way across the gorge, the sun slowly began to rise.

Finally, the last brick was set into place, and the project was complete. Six of the seven horsemen waved to Amir and Eva, and then rode off down the path into the desolate land below. Only The Great King remained, prepared to give his final words.

"When I was a child," he said, "I sincerely felt that it was my destiny to unite the world, and I spent my whole life trying. While I thought I was close at the time, it is now clear that I was far from reaching such lofty expectations. However, as I stand here today with the two of you, my ancient dream might come to pass.

"In the midst of your darkest hour, I hope I have helped to restore your faith. You must believe in the promise of The Great Mystery, for its promise will always be fulfilled."

"How can we possibly repay your people for the work they have done?" asked Amir. "This bridge is the greatest gift we could have ever asked for, let alone received."

"Do not forget," the king replied. "Never again will a night be as long and dark as this one. When the sun goes to sleep, and the moon fails to show, just look to the stars. There will be one for every person who has helped you build this bridge; and they will light your way on the darkest nights. The darker the night, the more you will see, until the day when you are with them once again."

For the third and final time, Alexander raised his polished sword high into the sky. This time though, Amir and Eva could see the reflection of the mysterious sentry on the blade. The lone rider still kept watch from the far side of the gorge.

"Don't worry friends," assured the king with a wink as he turned to ride away. "I won't tell my teacher what you did with his family's books."

Just then, Alexander called to his mighty horse before riding off into the distance. As they galloped swiftly down the path, Eva and Amir watched in silence, and awaited the miraculous winds.

As expected, they blew down fiercely from the cliffs, and chased the king from behind. However, the wind was unable to catch up, and Alexander the Great rode off on his mighty stallion, eventually disappearing around the bend in the path.

The longest night was over, and the dazzling sun now hovered directly overhead, punctuating the clear blue sky. As they turned to cross the bridge, they saw the lone rider and her three horses for the first time. Unable to utter a single word, they looked at one another in mutual understanding.

On the other side of the gorge, the most beautiful woman they had ever seen sat confidently on the middle of her three horses. Her amazing green eyes reflected the sun's vivid new light, and her dark hair blew wildly in the cool breeze, never once obstructing her face. For clothes, she wore a thin black dress, just as she had the night before.

CHAPTER
26

Though it had come to a timely end, the long and terrifying night had taken its toll on Amir and Eva. They had aged well into their thirties during the encounter with the warriors, but had learned invaluable lessons in the process. They had no doubt that their newfound appreciation for the efforts of others, would someday prove beneficial in uniting the world.

On the other hand, they were distraught with the idea that they were still aging very quickly. They could not imagine why The Great Mystery would have allowed such terror and oppression to reign upon the world, when the ultimate purpose was to save it. They could not comprehend why the wise people in the temple had offered their priceless books to irresponsible teenagers. Their uncertainties were testing their faith every step of the way. They doubted if they had truly been given the tools for a successful journey.

As they approached the end of the bridge, the beautiful woman and her three horses began riding up the path just ahead. They followed quietly behind for a while, never able to catch up. Then finally, Amir called out.

"Excuse me," he said.

The woman and her horses came to a rest on the path. Amir and Eva waited for a reply, but initially, there was none.

"Excuse me," Amir said again. "Aren't you the innkeeper?"

For an instant, silence lingered in the air. The woman arched her back slightly, slowly lifting her face to the sky. She stared into the blinding sun without a single blink. Her hair continued to blow in the wind, growing longer by the second. Streaks of grey appeared, and her skin aged significantly as they watched.

The woman lowered her eyes from the sun, slowly turning her head toward Amir and Eva. Her bright green eyes stared at each of them simultaneously. When she spoke, her once enchanting voice came out as an all too familiar whisper. The sound of her words came from everywhere at once.

"Why don't you ask what's really on your mind?" she asked, as she gave them a look they would never forget. "Come. Ride with me for a while, for you will never make it to the summit on your own."

Knowing the old woman's tremendous power, they listened without hesitation. Each of them climbed onto a horse, and continued their ascent of the great mountain. It was clear by the changing environment that they had entered the section of the trail that was hidden on the scroll: the treacherous northern face. As they rode side by side they came to understand The Great Mystery in a much deeper way than ever before.

While the woman had appeared mysterious upon their arrival at the inn, Eva and Amir had never suspected her true identity. Knowing there was no sense in doubting her enigmatic ways, they began to ask the troubling questions on their minds. Having not deciphered the message of the sacred books, they had developed some very crippling misunderstandings.

"Why have you chosen to deceive us?" Eva asked. "You said we would unite the world, yet your assistance has only slowed us down."

"I do not set the pace by which you travel," she answered. "I set the course. I am the law by which every choice will work itself out in time. I exist in a permanent state, unaffected by the process of change. Both Good and Evil are your own inventions, not mine. I do not pick sides or intervene. If I did, it would imply that I messed something up from the start. Such is not the case, I assure you."

"But you deceived us by pretending to be a younger woman," said Eva.

"How can one deceive, if she exists in everything? With the right perspective, you would see me everywhere. If you cannot imagine such things, then you are simply not prepared to unite the world. Please, do not blame me for your troubles, for I have already provided the tools with which you will succeed."

"How have you provided the tools?" Eva asked. "Everything you've given us has caused more trouble. The chest, the books, the cart, the scroll... each has led to the destruction of the world, and has left us much older in the process. This is no longer a world worth living in."

"But yet it is full of opportunity," the woman explained. "You must learn to accept responsibility for the way things are. You could have made it to the inn much faster, but you chose to carry the extra weight. In time, everything will play out, just as I have promised."

They lowered their eyes in embarrassment as she continued to reveal their misunderstanding.

"Think twice next time before assuming that material things are my gifts to you. Your bodies alone are the only vehicles needed to transport the promised tools. What is a fine wooden chest compared to the gift of life?"

Amir and Eva listened as they rode up the path. As it narrowed, the horses walked in line to avoid getting too close to the dangerous ledge. They moved gracefully around the icy north face of the mountain, protected by The Great Mystery.

"I became the universe to share my ways with others. The gift of life is your chance to practice my virtues. You exist in my image, though not in a way that you currently understand. Blame me for everything if you wish. However, in light of the secret treasure, such blame is self-incriminating. To this I will say no more.

"The treasure provides the answer that every human seeks. It alone is the reason for your insistent need to know why. What tool, aside from reason, would one need to find an answer?"

Eva and Amir considered the question, and realized their mistake. Their ability to ask questions and find answers was indeed the greatest tool in the world. It had allowed humans to unite families and nations, and to rule over the animal kingdom. *Perhaps it can enable us to unite the world too*, they thought, *but how?*

"The final answer which humans seek, cannot be found in the parts alone, but only in the whole. This is why you were asked to keep the books together. It was a test, and a lesson that you must learn before moving on. Yet even in your failure you have grown closer to the treasure.

"In war, people enhance their technologies. In sickness, they develop cures. Only having seen hate, can one fully appreciate true love.

"Like I said before, I do not pick sides, I just am. You must learn to see as I see, and teach this art to others. People must understand how every part works together for a greater purpose. There is order in the universe, but only the secret treasure will allow humankind to see it. Everything will make sense when it is finally discovered."

Amir and Eva now fully realized the mistake they had made in doubting the promises and wisdom of The Great Mystery, but she continued to speak as they crossed the north face.

"When this conversation is over, I will not reveal myself in this way until the treasure is found. When I leave, I will give you no more answers. By now, you should understand. I have offered you both help every step of the way, but you must learn to see this. You do have free will, but there is no choice you can make that will shield you from life's important lessons. In this way, your world is perfect. I have given you nothing but opportunity, time and time again."

"Know this; if there is breath in your lungs, you have not fulfilled your destiny. Until that day, you will follow the course I have set in place; a course that ensures both hardship and growth; to the end that all will know their natural place within the universe."

"I know you won't reveal the location of the secret treasure," said Eva, "but can you at least tell us if we're close?"

To this, the woman replied, "As I said in the forest when we first met, the treasure is close, but extremely hard to find. You are now as close as you have ever been."

Suddenly, the horses stopped. Looking around they realized they had crossed the entire northern face, and made their way to where the trail re-emerged on the scroll. *It will not be far to the summit from here*, they thought.

"This is as far as I can take you," said the woman. "I have carried you through the toughest part of the journey. From here, you must find the treasure on your own. I will see you both when your search is over."

Eva and Amir dismounted their horses. When they stood on solid ground, they realized that their energy had returned. Though they had aged well into their forties, a restored sense of hope made them feel much younger than before.

As Amir and Eva stood there on the path high up on the great mountain, the old woman and her three horses began to gallop on ahead toward the summit.

"Wait," yelled Eva as a final question came to mind.

The Great Mystery stopped just before disappearing around the bend in the trail up above. She did not speak, but looked back to hear the question.

"Are we doing the right thing by climbing the mountain?" Eva asked. "I feel like we've done more harm than good."

"It's all part of the grand design my dear," the woman replied. "Only by climbing the mountain, can you see the view from the top. From there, you will know my perspective."

As old Mother Nature rode her three horses around the corner, Amir and Eva hurried to ask more questions, but it was too late. She had disappeared yet again.

Having grown wiser from the conversation, they still had no idea what they were looking for, or where it would be. *Close by, but hard to find*, she had said.

The summit was near, and they now had the energy to find it. With the understanding that no one had been there before, Eva and Amir marched on in hope that they would be the first.

However, as they turned the bend in the trail, only one thing occupied their attention. It was not the spectacular view to the west, or the frigid air blowing all around. Instead of the summit, or a treasure of any kind, there was a much more puzzling sight.

As it turned out, they would not be the first to ascend the great mountain after all.

CHAPTER
27

Eva and Amir approached what seemed to be the end of the path. The only problem was that they were nowhere near the summit. They hardly had time to consider their options before noticing something even more puzzling. At the trail's end, a large metal door had been built into the rocky wall. The cold, stainless-steel door was sealed air tight, and locked from within. A tiny video camera was mounted in the upper-right corner, protruding from the rock. While Eva had no idea what it was, she did notice the small red light, which began glowing when they first stepped in front of the door.

"Wow," exclaimed Eva, "this is incredible!" She examined every inch of the area, trying to figure out a way in.

"Yes," replied Amir, suddenly not feeling so well. "It sure is something, isn't it?"

Eva noticed the unusual fatigue in Amir's voice, and was immediately concerned. "Are you feeling alright?"

But Amir was getting dizzy, and did not hear the question. He leaned into the cold door with one hand, attempting to regain his balance. Though he stood still, the world seemed to spin slowly around him. He looked down, and then tried closing his eyes, but nothing seemed to help.

"Eva," he said, barely able to speak. "There's something..." but he stopped short of finishing, now hardly able to breathe.

Not sure of what to say, Eva put her hand on his shoulder and tried to help.

"Maybe you should sit down for a minute," she said, tilting her head to see his sunken face. "You're not looking so good right now."

Amir became increasingly weak. He turned his back to the wall and slid down until he was sitting on the ground. The world continued to spin, making him nauseous.

"Is there anything I can do?" asked Eva, unsure of what had suddenly come over him.

"I feel weak," Amir said softly. "I'm pretty sure it's...," but before he could finish, his world went dark and quiet. His torso slumped over, and he fell to the stone path.

Eva was now scared, and dropped to a knee to shake his arm.

"Amir!" she yelled, trying desperately to bring him back. "Wake up Amir! Wake up!" But he did not move.

Eva rested her hand on her lifeless friend, and began to sob. Her own life flashed before her eyes. Everything she had envisioned of the future, changed in that instant.

CHAPTER
28

Eva spun around and leaned into the cold steel door, then dropped to the ground beside Amir's motionless body. She covered her face with her hands, trying to hold back the oncoming flood of emotion. Her breaths became shallow as she contemplated their long journey's tragic end. A tear welled up in her eye and then began to slide down her cheek. Having left a thin glossy streak on her face, it paused at her chin, and dropped to the ground.

For an instant, Eva thought she had heard the tear hitting the ground. Then she realized the sound had come from above. In the upper corner of the doorway, the camera was moving slowly in her direction, but then it stopped. The tiny red light shined right into her teary eyes, blinked a few times...and went dark.

Just then, Eva was frightened by an incredible hissing noise. She leaned forward to cover Amir as steam suddenly billowed from the door. She could barely see in the fog. For the moment, everyone was invisible, hidden by the surrounding mist. She stayed close to his body, knowing there was nowhere else to go.

Strange voices filled the area, getting louder as they closed in. Someone suddenly grabbed her by the arm and pulled her to her feet.

"I'll check on the girl," shouted an unfamiliar female voice. "Take him directly to medical."

Eva was dumbfounded. *What was medical?* she thought. *Where are they taking Amir?*

The mist began to dissipate, allowing Eva to see for the first time. Strange people in green linen scrubs were loading Amir onto a stretcher; then strapping him down. Next to Eva stood the woman in command of the situation, the one with the unfamiliar voice.

"Please, get up and come with me," she calmly requested. "How do you know the man on the floor?"

Eva thought briefly about all they had been through.

"He is my best friend," Eva said sadly. "His name is Amir."

"Wonderful, my name is Nadia," the woman replied with a brilliant smile. "It's a pleasure to finally meet you."

The woman continued to grin as she invited a very confused Eva through the open doorway, and into the mountain.

Finally, thought Nadia, *the Chosen Ones have returned.*

CHAPTER
29

Eva had not been separated from Amir since their initial encounter in the jungles of their homeland. But now, high on the great mountain, they were being taken to separate areas of a sophisticated alpine fortress.

The mist cleared as the steel door closed, sealing off the frigid outside air from the much warmer interior of the complex. Eva tried her best to keep up as they traveled briskly down a long windowless hall toward an undisclosed location.

Nadia was tall and thin, but well toned. She had light hazel eyes, smooth brown skin, and shimmering black hair. She wore a slender white jacket and bright red calf length pants. On her feet, she wore brown leather clogs without socks, leaving her heals exposed.

"We're so glad that you finally found us," said Nadia in a friendly, but authoritative tone. "There are some people I would like you to meet. They've been anticipating your arrival for quite some time."

"Where have you taken my friend?" Eva asked, not quite able to trust the woman. "What will be done to him?"

Nadia slowed her pace for a moment as she thought of how to explain without revealing too much. Before entering the polished mahogany door at the end of the hallway, she stopped, took hold of Eva's hands, and tried to calm her fears.

"Eva," she said calmly, "I know this is a strange place for you right now. You won't understand everything immediately, but you must trust that we have your best interest in mind. It is because of us that you are here."

They left the map? Eva realized. *But I thought...*

"Your friend is currently in the hands of the finest medical team in the world. There's nothing you can do for him now, but he'll be fine. You'll see him shortly."

He's alive, thought Eva... *impossible.*

"First though, you must meet a few people who can better explain your present situation, and hopefully your future."

Eva was unsure how to respond, but her fear dissipated at the sound of Nadia's calming voice. While worried for Amir's health, she had no doubt that he was better off now than he would have been. It was, after all, these people who had found him lying unconscious on the icy path outside. Eva had assumed the worst for Amir, but now it seemed he might be ok. She experienced an awkward mix of anxiety and hope as she awaited her uncertain future.

As Nadia reached for the shimmering golden door handle, Eva caught a glimpse of an engraving on the knob. The woman's hand grasped the fixture before Eva could make out anything specific. Though unable to make a certain connection in time, her mind had been triggered.

Somewhere in the midst of her sub-conscious, a faint light came on. Chills ran briefly through her body, causing the hair on her arms to rise.

Nadia opened the large wooden door. "Well, here we are," she said.

Eva attempted to get another glimpse of the doorknob on her way into the lobby, but Nadia intentionally kept it hidden.

One thing is for sure, she thought as they entered the large room. *The design of that door bared an uncanny resemblance to the infamous mahogany chest.*

CHAPTER
30

The amazing mountain fortress was unlike anything Eva could have imagined. On the inside of the impressive mahogany door, was the grand lobby. The room had been designed as a large half-circle. The dark brown, wide-panel, hardwood floor shined as if recently polished. The curved exterior was a solid section of glass, providing both light and a panoramic view of the spectacular landscape to the west. The twenty-foot high, polished stone walls of the interior gave the room a museum like quality. Colorful minerals were swirled within the grey stone, like a rainbow, trapped within the smooth rock. In the center of the room, two black leather couches faced one another, separated by a luxurious slate coffee table. On the table was a single book with leather binding and gold-leaf pages. It resembled the sacred books of the temple, but Eva knew better after what had happened.

Eva walked silently over to the window. As she neared the glass, she could hardly believe what she saw. Built into the side of the towering granite peak, were hundreds of structures, each one carved neatly into the mountain itself. Astonishingly, the snow and ice did not accumulate within the village, and the surface appeared warm and dry. Around the windows, there were vines and flourishing flowerpots, somehow defying the deadly altitude. The natural appearance of the buildings must have camouflaged them from anyone looking up at the mountain from far below.

The setting sun neared the horizon, but was still high enough to provide full light on the area to the west. The land was pristine and without the scars of the violent struggle that had taken place in the east. What Eva had once thought of as the whole world, had doubled in an instant. The problems they had encountered in previous days appeared insignificant in light of all that could now be seen. Far below, the waters sparkled in the waning sunlight, and the forests, fields, and hills appeared untouched by humanity.

After taking in the view for a moment and considering the origins of the mysterious alpine civilization, Eva noticed the woman waiting patiently on the other side of the room. The central portion of the far wall had opened, revealing a sophisticated elevator compartment. Nadia stood in the doorway and called to Eva.

"Please, join me when you're ready," she requested. "The council will have much to discuss with you."

Eva glanced once more at the scene outside the windows before turning and walking to the elevator. While passing the furniture in the middle of the room, she once again noticed the book sitting on the table. The cover contained a circular design, but she could not make out anything more from her distance. She hurried to meet Nadia on the elevator.

The doors closed smoothly, sealing them inside. Nadia pressed her thumb to a laser scanner and watched as the once dark panel on the back wall turned into a large digital map.

"This is where we are now," she said as she pointed, "and this is where we're going."

The map was a side shot of the complex within the mountain. As Nadia pressed her finger to the screen, it came to life. The image rotated to reveal a top-down look at the highest level of the fortress. It appeared to be a single small room near the summit. She tapped the image of their apparent destination, and a digital keyboard appeared, prompting them for an additional security code.

Evidently, access to the top floor is granted only to the elite, Eva thought.

Nadia typed in a random thirteen-character password, and then hit submit. They waited for a few seconds until the message flashed briefly on the screen, *access granted*. The elevator began to rise slowly.

Eva had an uneasy sensation as they arose. The advanced civilization was unlike anything she could have imagined. Their technology made them appear like gods. Every aspect of the long journey had led her to the now approaching summit. However it had happened, someone wanted the treasure to be found, or perhaps even had it already. Though possibly on the verge of fulfilling The Great Mystery's promise, something seemed out of place. It was not supposed to happen without Amir. Suddenly, she felt ill with worry for her friend's health and safety.

"Is everything alright dear?" asked Nadia.

"Not really," Eva replied. "This should be an exciting moment, but I never envisioned it this way. Amir and I were supposed to find this place together."

"Ah," Nadia sighed as the elevator slowed, "but you did. You must trust that your friend is ok. How will we trust you, if you cannot trust us?"

Her words hung on Eva's ears for a moment. It seemed that she had once heard the same phrase elsewhere, perhaps even on this very mountain. Could it be that Nadia too was The Great Mystery in disguise? Though it seemed plausible for an instant, Eva reminded herself not to speculate. She focused her mind on the present, and thought hard about what she could learn from her current circumstances.

"I do trust you Nadia," Eva said. "I just don't feel complete without him. That's all."

"That's good to know," Nadia replied. "I'm pretty sure he feels the same about you."

The elevator stopped... the doors slowly opened... Eva and Nadia had arrived.

CHAPTER
31

Eva stepped off the elevator, and into an empty, windowless room. She expected Nadia to follow, but the elevator doors began to shut almost instantly. She reached out to halt the closing doors, but stopped when she saw the woman smiling back.

"Pay attention up here," Nadia advised, "the treasure is within reach, and your world needs you to find it."

The doors closed, leaving Eva alone in the dimly lit room. She instantly felt as if she'd been deceived, and tried desperately to pry the elevator open. Unfortunately, it was sealed tight, and the doors did not budge. She pounded with her fists on it, angry about being abandoned so late in the journey.

"What do I do now?" she yelled at the doors. Her voice echoed in the room until it faded away, never reaching Nadia's ears.

She screamed once again in frustration, "What kind of place is this?"

There were no buttons or handles to summon the elevator's return. Eva was trapped. She looked to the ceiling and closed her eyes, trying to imagine where she had gone wrong. *We must have missed something*, she thought, but nothing came to mind. She opened her eyes and stared at the sealed doors.

Then, while on the verge of total despair, a voice called out to her from behind.

"Can I help you find something ma'am?" a deep male voice asked.

Eva was startled, and turned to see who it was. An opening in the stone wall opposite from the elevator revealed an old man with white hair and aged skin. His light-blue eyes glowed within the dimly lit room. He wore a dark suit and tie. Eva stared in shock.

"Why don't you come with me Eva," the man said. "My friends and I have a lot of explaining to do."

Eva was unsure of how the old man knew her name, but she followed his instruction. As she approached, he stepped to the side and raised his left arm, motioning for her to go first.

She wanted to ask him a million questions, but she got the feeling that questions would not be necessary. Rather than speak, she walked silently past him toward the spiral staircase that climbed to the next level. Light emanated from above. There was nowhere to go but up.

She climbed the stairs with her eyes glued to the opening in the ceiling. She could see the clouds through a circular window above the stairs. The remaining sunlight was enough to reveal an engraving on the glass, but it was impossible to make out anything specific.

Eva and the old man emerged into a private meeting room by way of an opening in the floor. As they entered from below, Eva instantly realized the significance of the situation. She was standing in the center of a circular table exactly like the one in the temple. Men and women, sat around the table. Some wore white lab coats, and others finely tailored suits. Only one seat was empty.

A floor to ceiling glass window, providing unobstructed views in all directions, enclosed the moderately sized circular room. The ceiling was painted black, but the glass opening in the center provided additional light over the table. The overhead window was not stained glass as it had been in the temple, but clear, creating the illusion of the sun shining through the night. *Perhaps*, Eva thought, *the lost understanding of humankind will be revealed in this symbolic room.*

Eva spun in a circle, amazed at the surrounding views. She had never seen the world from such an inclusive perspective. From there in the meeting room, her world looked much different. No borders could be seen between one nation and another. She knew there was only one explanation; she had arrived at the summit.

Though it wasn't at all what she expected, there was nowhere else to go. The scroll had indeed been a map, and she had reached her destination. The treasure had to be close. All she needed was Amir.

The old man left her standing in the center of the table, and walked around the room. After taking in the view for a moment, he stood by the lone empty chair, in front of the setting sun. Before sitting, he spoke to Eva.

"My name is Isaac Newton," he said. "Welcome to the Council of Science."

CHAPTER
32

Eva was shocked to have made it into the council without Amir. The Great Mystery had clearly indicated their need for one another. She also feared that without his wisdom, they might miss something important, and fail to find the treasure. Soon, she would understand.

The sun set beyond the hills, and the night sky lit up with stars, reminding her of Alexander's message at the bridge. Darkness swallowed the land far below, and tiny lights dotted the landscape like stars on the ground. The technology of the mountain fortress spread like wildfires throughout the world as she watched.

Eva stood with the Council of Science, needing to learn a few more important things.

"I know you're worried about Amir," said Isaac. As he spoke, four rectangular panels of transparent glass descended from the ceiling, one in each direction. "Please direct your attention to the monitors as I explain."

The screens came to life with a spectacular three-dimensional display. The colors on the monitor reminded Eva of Amir's attire when they had first met in the woods. Never before had she seen such bright colors, except in nature. Eva still held to the hope that it was just an odd coincidence, though she could not have been further from the truth.

On the monitors, a live video feed connected them to an operating room somewhere within the compound. Eva was horrified by what she saw. She raised her hand to her mouth as she gasped. Unable to speak, she watched the robotic arms operating on her friend. At the controls, a masked surgeon sat nearby. Her mind had no way of knowing what was going on. As far as she knew, Amir was being tortured with unimaginable cruelty.

Amir was on his back, lying on a table. His body was mostly covered in blue cloth, but his torso and face were clearly visible. Dotted lines on his chest were being cut by the machine's spinning blade. Tubes and wires connected him to other devices nearby, which seemed to be prolonging his suffering. Remarkably, he was completely still and quiet. When the machine had finished cutting through his chest, the saw was removed. Tiny claws then gripped each side of his severed sternum. They pulled it apart, revealing a mass of fleshy insides. There, in plain sight, was Amir's beating heart. Eva turned away, unable to watch any longer. She stared Isaac in the eyes, doubtful that any explanation would suffice.

Isaac waited patiently for her to speak, but she couldn't. He noticed her fear turning to anger. Then, as she was about to speak, he interrupted.

"Eva," he said, "your friend Amir is going to be fine. He's in an operating room nearby. I know this may seem like science fiction to you right now, but it's very real. He's having open-heart surgery to replace his aortic valve. The surgeons in that room are the best around. When they're finished, he'll be sewn up. The two of you will be together again soon. However, he must remain in isolation until the surgery is over. It's a necessity to prevent infection."

Eva didn't know what to say. In just a few days, she had aged nearly forty-five years, traveled from her primitive homeland to a sophisticated mountain complex, and met some of the most influential people of all time. Until now, all she had cared about was the treasure at the end, but seeing her friend in such a condition made her wonder if it had all been worth it.

Isaac continued to explain. "Amir is fast asleep. When he awakens, he will not remember any of this. It's called anesthesia. The substance has assisted greatly with surgical capabilities in modern times."

"I don't understand why I'm here anymore," Eva said. "I thought there was some kind of treasure. The mysterious old woman assured us it was here. She said that once we found it, we could unite the entire world."

"And the problem is?" asked Isaac.

"Obviously, there's no treasure here. Even if there was, I can't possibly lead a world that is so advanced beyond my own."

"Take a look around you child," Isaac said. "This is the same world that you came from, just a different part. You are only seeing it from a new perspective. We live in a big place, but we can't see it all at once. What we can do is understand how it all works, and live in harmony with its inherent natural laws. Your simple village, the wars, the temple, and this complex all exist in different parts of the same world. What we do not see still affects us.

"The treasure will reveal the truth about how we're all connected. All humans can live peacefully together, but we must first learn to live in harmony with ourselves. Until then, we will all suffer the illnesses brought on by a lack of balance."

If the world is already united, Eva thought, *then what's the point of this journey?*

"The treasure you seek is close by, but hard to find. Am I right?" he asked.

"So I've been told," Eva responded, surprised that he spoke those exact words.

"Then why have you traveled to the top of this mountain to find it?" asked Isaac. It was an obvious question that Eva had not yet considered.

"We found a map on a scroll," she explained. "Then we followed it up the mountain. We had some strange experiences, learned some valuable lessons, and eventually made our way up here. That's the what happened, though it was actually a bit more complicated."

"It was complicated because we made it that way," Isaac explained. "It was us who left the scroll and the clothing. It was us who spoke to you in the temple, advised you at the inn, and built you a bridge to cross the gorge. We have done these things, one life at a time, to guide others here to this room. We did not specifically have you in mind, but we set it all up as an attempt to find leaders for our new world."

"New world?" Eva asked, unsure of what he had meant by the phrase. "How did you know anyone would figure it all out? How can you sit up here and watch while the world struggles, knowing that you have the answer to fix it all?"

Eva could never have guessed how astonishing his answer would be.

CHAPTER 33

"Well, if you must know now," Isaac said, "I'll try to explain.

"A long time ago, on a distant planet known as Earth, we witnessed the very same struggles time and time again. We fought to control them for centuries, trying to find a solution that would bring peace to the world. However, while some searched for harmony, others thrived on greed and power. In the field of technology, we advanced at astounding speed, but our full potential could never be realized. The citizens of Earth did not understand their inherent unity. They did not possess the secret treasure.

"Though many good ideas were born in the minds of our people, we could not put the pieces together until it was too late. Injustice, hate, and greed deprived us of our vital resources. Famine and disease plagued the Earth as we gradually returned to the tribal societies from which we grew. It was a trying time, but we learned a lot about ourselves.

"In fact, a few of us discovered an exciting truth about humanity in the waning hours of hope. That truth became known as the secret treasure. It held the power to unite our entire race with mutual purpose and understanding. With it, we could guide humankind toward the realization of our maximum potential. In light of the treasure, we could prove the true nature of all existence: that our universe is, and always has been, The Kingdom of God."

Eva didn't quite know what to think. She had seen mention of such a kingdom in the sacred books, but thought it was far away, if not a complete fantasy. *Could people just like her and Amir actually have come from elsewhere in the universe?* She thought. *Could such a treasure even be possible?* She had her doubts, but Isaac continued to explain.

"A team of leaders from many nations came together as human life on Earth neared its end. In desperation, they developed highly advanced aerospace machines using the sacred books of knowledge. These books were held in secrecy, where only the wise could read them, and they contained every ounce of scientific and spiritual wisdom ever discovered.

"With no time for chances, they could not risk letting such knowledge into the hands of greedy villains, so they kept the treasure hidden. They pleaded with tribal groups to find common ground, but no one would listen.

"Knowing that other worlds existed, the team set out into space to find a new start. Those who were able to escape continued to study the sacred texts. They taught their children to understand the metaphoric language of God: The Great Mystery, which had become the universe. Generation after generation, they developed greater intelligence until even the children possessed superhuman wisdom. In contrast to life on Earth, it was much easier to see how the actions of one affected the whole while living in such small quarters.

"Finally, after many generations had lived among the stars, they discovered a suitable planet, very similar to the one they had left behind. They landed here on this mountain, and disassembled their spacecraft in order to recreate their technologies on land. Inspired by the beautiful new world, and the volcanic mountain upon which they settled, they created legends to inspire their children. Through their own creativity, they preserved nature's inherent wisdom for future generations.

"One such legend likened this great mountain to life itself. While it may be very beautiful and peaceful at first glance, it is actually a dangerous volcano, capable of erupting at any moment. Our lives are equally unpredictable, and our plans are just as fragile. Lessons like this have kept the people focused on what was important: enjoying life, and supporting their community."

Eva silently considered the legend of the volcano, and saw how such lessons could impact one's attitude toward living.

"After a while, however, their sophisticated lifestyle became hard to sustain, and they chose to leave the mountain in search of simpler ways to live. Eventually, they settled in a land between the two great rivers. They called the land Mesopotamia in remembrance of the first civilizations on Earth.

"Ancient stories of struggles on Earth led them to the understanding that simpler was indeed better. The secret treasure gave them peace of mind, mutual purpose, and unity. They conquered their impulsive desires by keeping the well-being of others in mind. They had truly mastered themselves, and the art of living happily."

"So what happened?" Eva asked. "It seems they had it all figured out?"

"Everything changes my friend, and no one escapes the process. Only the cycle itself is constant. Only by acknowledging the way life is, can we ever grow stronger as a whole."

"Where are they now?" she replied. "I am from the land that you speak of, and I have never met such advanced people before."

"Well, the further they moved from the mountain, the simpler life became. As an unintended consequence, they gradually lost touch with the knowledge of their secret treasure. They took it for granted, and it vanished.

"While they ventured from the mountain with great wisdom, they failed to pass it on to their children, and it was gone within a few generations. As the years went by, they grew further from the truth, just like the busy civilizations of Earth. The process simply worked backwards here. They started with technological advancement, and ran away from it, thereby failing to diagnose the dreaded infection of greed."

"I don't understand," replied Eva. "How is looking for a simpler life considered greedy?"

"The Guardians of the treasure failed to share the secret knowledge with others. They thought it would be misused, but without it, there was no shared purpose by which to live. Sure, they hid clues within their myths, but when the parents stopped teaching the metaphoric language to their children, they could no longer decipher the secret messages within the myths.

"Later generations saw the stories as lies, or at best, childish. They sought facts instead of legends, and searched for truth in the world around them. The problem was that truth was not around them, but within them, a place we rarely look. The treasure eludes even the brightest minds, while remaining nearby at all times...just as you were told."

With her limited knowledge of human anatomy and physiology, Eva did not quite understand how the body itself could contain secrets for uniting the world, but she would find out soon enough.

"Eventually, only two Guardians remained, and they lived here in this complex as the chosen rulers of the world. They protected the treasure, just as generations of Guardians had done before them. However, as they grew in age, they were faced with a great dilemma."

"So how does this involve me and Amir?" questioned Eva.

"The Guardians were very old, and feared what might happen to the treasure if they died without an heir. The only hope was their five-year-old son. His life story was a legend in itself."

It can't be, Eva thought as she put the pieces together in her mind.

"An infant boy had been abandoned at the foot of the great mountain, left in the wilderness to die as an orphan. The compassionate Guardians found him there while hunting, and brought him in. They took care of him as their own, but the boy became very sick.

"He suffered from a congenital heart defect, and was not expected to live until his next birthday. As if this wasn't enough to disqualify him from the throne, he was also much too young to rule the world, leaving the Guardians without much hope."

"Why didn't they just teach him about the treasure?" Eva asked.

"The treasure is only useful when combined with wisdom," replied Isaac. "If I give a bag of seeds to a man who has never gone hungry, he will most likely throw them away. But given to the wise person who has suffered starvation, those same seeds can change the world."

"I see," she replied. "The boy was not wise, and the others had fled the mountain in search of a simpler life. It's just a shame that there wasn't another way."

"Ah yes, but the story never ends my dear," the scientist replied. "As the boy neared his final days, a very dangerous procedure was performed to try and save him. During the operation, the world stood still. His damaged heart was replaced, and he survived. The recovery was long and painful, but the healing process helped him to identify life's real treasures, and see the world from an enlightened perspective.

"To the Guardians, the boy's predicament was a good omen, and they saw him as the living example of their volcano legend. He would always be reminded of the importance of paying attention to the present, and the imminence of death would drive him to live well. In the days following the surgery, this proved to be true, and he became wise much faster than normal."

"So he was able to save the day then. Right?" Eva asked, now tuned into the story, as if it was her own.

"The treasure has never been left in the possession of one man alone. In a world dependent upon both male and female contributions for survival, it has been a rule to have at least one of each in command. This is to ensure that the needs of all people are met, with both equal attention and resolve. In addition, it gets lonely on top of the world, and everyone needs a companion."

"So you're telling me that they didn't trust the boy?" Eva said.

"That's not what I am saying at all," Isaac replied. "They were protecting him, and did not want to put the weight of the world on his shoulders alone."

"Then what happened to the Guardians, and their child?" Eva begged.

"Well," he began, "As the legend goes, the boy's mother was visited one night by a mysterious older woman. A woman with eyes so bright, that they glowed in the darkness."

Eva stopped breathing for a moment and covered her mouth with her hands, unable to hide the connection she had made in her mind.

"The boy's family was given a choice. First, of course, they could choose to remain atop the mountain, protecting their treasure for the rest of their lives. Or, they could leave their treasure behind, part ways with the advanced alpine complex, and move with the boy into the wilderness down below."

"Why would anyone choose to leave this place, or to give up the secret treasure?" Eva asked.

"Why else?" replied Newton. "Because the old woman promised something in return."

"Like what?" she asked, anxious to hear the rest.

"That the boy would return with a worthy partner, and that they would find the treasure once again."

Eva suddenly knew why Nadia had welcomed her to the compound.

That boy, of course... was her friend Amir.

CHAPTER
34

The sun had been down for half the night when the robotic machine finally began to sew Amir's chest back together. His sternum was replaced with a metal plate, and the outer skin was reattached with surgical glue to reduce scarring. Amazingly, Eva noticed his arm moving on the video monitor just a short while later. Her friend was alive.

As Amir recovered and the doctors allowed the anesthesia to wear off, Isaac introduced the other members of the Scientific Council.

"I would like to direct your attention to the monitors once again," Isaac gestured. The streaming images of Amir in the operating room were replaced by a three-dimensional logo of The Vitruvian Man. The image rotated on the screen, begging for Eva to recognize its significance to her quest.

"While we cannot reveal the secret treasure itself, we will do our very best to help you understand."

"May I sit down?" asked Eva. "This might take a while, and I'm exhausted."

"Life is difficult by design," answered Isaac. "If you wish to unite the world, you cannot do it sitting down. You must move about in order to see the needs of your people. They must learn from your actions before they will hear your words. Your people must see the power of the treasure through your belief. There is a great difference between one who advises others, and one who believes. Do you know what that difference is?"

"Not exactly," she replied.

"Anyone can give advice despite their own integrity," he continued, "but such advice most often falls on deaf ears. If I believe something, then I apply it to my own life with faith that it will work. I do not stray from it, because I know it is true. If I should stray, then I simply did not fully believe in the first place."

"Okay," Eva said, "but I don't understand. Is there something specific that I need to believe in?"

"Of course there is," answered Isaac. "You have been searching for it. When your people look to you for reassurance during hard times, they must know that you believe in what you offer them. If you have doubts, they will have no faith. Not everyone is meant to lead, but all have an equally important role to play. As a leader, you will be their image on the scroll. Your people will look to you and follow your actions, good or bad. They will follow you up the mountain of life, so that they too can reach their destiny."

"But I can't be perfect," she said.

"You will never be '*perfect*' by your definition, but you are merely a small part of a much bigger design. You must learn to see the world from a different perspective, and accept that your flaws are not always what they seem. While you alone will surely fall short of the people's expectations, the truth will never let them down."

Now fully understanding that there would be no easy answers, Eva accepted the challenge and watched as the old man seated next to Isaac stood. He pushed in his chair, and walked slowly around the table. The wise man from Vinci introduced himself before teaching one of his most beloved lessons: The Anatomy and Physiology of the Human Body.

CHAPTER
35

From one system to the next, Eva listened intently as the virtual images on the screens supplemented Leonardo's fascinating explanations of how the human body operated. He talked about how each part worked to support the whole, and how that whole would suffer from the loss or malfunction of any one part. He also explained the vital organs, and the body's inherent capacity to fight off certain diseases and infections. Other members in the room joined in at times to expound on the psychological and social aspects of what they called, "The Human Machine".

Upon completion of how the body worked in ideal situations, they moved on to the ways in which it could be harmed, or even brought to an end. They went over the problem with Amir's heart in great detail, and closed by reviewing their recent advancements in medical research and technology.

Eva absorbed the lessons like a sponge, and learned everything down to the cellular level. She asked no questions during the lecture, but only listened. The Human Machine was more magnificent than she could have ever imagined. Of all the beautiful things she had ever seen, she knew for certain that this design was the most spectacular. As strange as it seemed, the workings of the body seemed nearly identical to the workings of the universe itself.

Leonardo made some closing comments before returning to his chair. The image of the slow spinning Vitruvian Man graphic once again appeared on the monitor. It changed colors as it rotated on the otherwise clear glass screens. Eva was left with a moment of silence to ponder the implications of what she had learned.

As she stood in the center of the table with thoughts racing through her mind, the monitors ascended back into the ceiling and disappeared. Once again, the attention seemed to focus entirely on the center of the room.

"I assume you have some questions," Isaac said. "Unfortunately, you do not have the time for us to answer them all. When the sun rises in the east, we will vanish as the light fills this room. You may ask one final question of us before we go."

"Please, I need more time to think," Eva begged.

"Don't worry," Newton explained. "The sun will not rise until we answer your question."

Unaware of what she was about to do, Eva asked the most immediate question on her mind. "How can you know when the sun will rise?"

Isaac interlocked his fingers and placed his hands on the table, appearing suddenly disappointed. "We have made many discoveries in our time," he answered. "Predicting a sun rise is about as simple as it gets. I hoped you would have used your question more wisely."

Eva could not believe it. The council members each stood up and pushed their chairs under the table. The situation felt eerily akin to their last moments in the temple.

Eva could feel the sun's heat as it edged close to the horizon. The morning sky began to glow with a reddish-purple haze, erasing all but the brightest stars from the canopy overhead. She closed her eyes with shame, and waited for the council to disappear. She knew that Amir would be disappointed when he found out what she had asked with her final question.

Then, as the sun's rays began to pierce the room through the glass, the scientists around the table gradually became transparent...except for one. Standing in the East, directly in front of the rising sun, was Albert Einstein. He offered one final explanation before departing with the council.

"Have no fear," whispered the wise scientist, "for the sun does not rise and fall like you might think."

Eva did not fully understand his advanced knowledge of the cosmos, and was unsure of the significance of his message. However, she listened as he finished, simply thankful that he offered more.

"It is not the sun, but those who depend on it, that rise and fall. The sun remains, and has the best interest of your whole rotating planet in mind. You must learn to think like the sun. The treasure that you seek is not new. It is a revelation of the way things have always been."

The sun appeared to rise higher in the sky until Einstein no longer blocked its rays. As the council vanished, the fading scientist whispered one last phrase. His voice echoed around the room.

"The sun may not rise and fall as you once thought," the voice explained, "but it does exist."

He then disappeared into the thin alpine air, replaced by the light of a brand new day.

CHAPTER
36

With the council now gone, Eva stood alone in the summit chamber. She exited the center of the table and made her way to the windows that encircled the room. The landscape had transformed dramatically overnight.

Eva moved slowly around the glass walled perimeter, taking note of the evolution that had taken place outside. She could see for miles in every direction, and immediately made connections between the world and what Leonardo had taught. For what it seemed, humans were unconsciously recreating the world in their own image.

Signal towers connected one place to another like society's central nervous system, constantly processing the world's information. Roads and tracks ran everywhere, serving as the veins and arteries by which people moved from one place to the next. Just like the immune system, law enforcement and military acted to rid the world of criminal infections, and the diseases of poverty and injustice.

She continued to note the similarities in her mind as she paced around the room, looking out at the ever-changing world. Then, having lost track of time, she was startled by the sound of footsteps coming up the stairs.

Amir emerged from the stairway looking slightly older, but refreshed. The color had returned to his face, and he had regained his edge. He looked around the room, expecting to see someone other than Eva.

"No treasure I assume," he said.

Eva was not sure how to respond to his comment. She wondered if he had been deceiving her the entire time, pretending not to know where he was going. At the same time however, they had become good friends, and she desperately wanted to trust him.

"Nothing yet," she replied. "Where have you been? I've been worried sick."

"Well, I had to take care of a little problem with my heart," Amir teased. "Maybe you could give me a break."

She was surprised that he came right out with the truth. "Why didn't you tell me the truth about your family?" asked Eva.

"You never asked," answered Amir.

"It seems like an important thing not to mention," Eva said. "You could have saved me a lot of worry."

"Perhaps I could've saved you the worry," replied Amir, "but the goal was to find the treasure, and I don't know where it is anymore than you do."

"So what do we do now?" she asked.

"What did you learn from the council?"

Eva was stunned. She had no idea how Amir knew about the council meeting. He had been in surgery the whole time.

"How could you know about the meeting?" Eva asked.

"Strange things happen when you're under anesthesia," said Amir. "You wouldn't believe me if I told you."

"Have you looked outside lately?" she asked, pointing to the windows. "Everything is evolving so fast. It's amazing."

"Once we find the treasure, everything should slow down. The people just need one thing before they will slow down and enjoy life. There is no peace, without peace of mind."

Something in Amir's last words triggered Eva's own mind.

"What did you just say?" she asked with a sudden deeper interest.

"I said that once we find..."

"Not that part," she interrupted, "the last part."

"About the mind?" he asked.

"Yes, that was it. What did you say about it?"

Amir began to see where she was going. "There is no peace without peace of mind," he said again. "It's something my parents used to say when I was a child."

Eva noted during the lecture that the mind was the most powerful tool of the human body. Without it, all other parts would be rendered quite useless. In fact, unless a conscious effort was made by the mind to use the body productively, there was little hope for a human to accomplish much good at all.

"Did you mean anything else by that?" she asked, feeling like he was hiding something of the utmost importance.

"Not really," answered Amir. "Why? What else would I have meant?"

At that moment, Amir covered his eyes with his hands to shield the sunlight, which had just peaked overhead. The light shined through the ceiling with intensity. Amir had to move from the center of the room due to the blinding light and increased heat.

Eva saw shade lines crossing rapidly across his body as he moved away, but they disappeared as soon as he moved from the light. It was then that she remembered the engraving on the window above. She had noticed it briefly upon entering the room.

As Amir moved, Eva approached to investigate. She squeezed by him as they traded places, and made her way toward the top of the spiral staircase. Amir was surprised by her sudden burst of energy and excitement.

At first, she looked up, attempting to see the outline on the glass, but was temporarily blinded by the sun's glow. Eva closed her eyes and looked away, shielding her face from the bright light. After losing her balance, she fell to a knee, and nearly tumbled into the opening below. She regained her composure, but did not stand back up. Instead, Eva lowered herself to the ground, and peered into the stairwell. She couldn't believe what she saw.

Amir scrambled over to help, kneeling down beside her. "Are you alright?" he asked with great concern for his friend.

Eva did not answer. She only pointed to the ground below.

CHAPTER
37

Now lying face down at the top of the spiral staircase, Eva was staring in wonder at the floor down below. She was too shocked to notice Amir's voice.

On the floor of the room below, the overhead sun had illuminated a circular area near the base of the stairs. Within the circle of light, was the image of an outstretched human figure. Its arms and legs reached desperately for the darkness surrounding the circle, but could not escape the encompassing light.

"Get over here," exclaimed Eva, "you have to see this!"

Amir moved carefully around her awkwardly sprawled body to position himself for a look. As he leaned in and peaked through the railing, he saw it too.

The Vitruvian Man stared up at them from the floor, hinting even more at what they were now gradually figuring out. Amir helped Eva to her feet, and they hurried down the stairs to get a better look. It was a perfect image, but the sun had no intentions of letting them stare at it for long.

As the sun slowly passed over the window in the ceiling of the room above, the image faded like the cycling moon in the night sky. They tried desperately to find clues before the image was gone.

A third of the image turned to shadow...then half... They watched as it faded before their eyes; only a sliver of light remained. Then, after only a moment of visibility, the symbolic human design was gone.

Having not discovered a single clue, Amir became frustrated. His health had provided him with a window into life's soul that few could ever know. At times however, such a perspective made patience hard to come by. He was growing tired of waiting, and worried that the prime of his life was passing him by as they searched in vain for the elusive secret treasure. He took out the scroll and rushed up the stairs. Eva followed... as he knew she would.

He put the scroll on the table, and they went over the details of their quest. They had taken the only path. They had met with the three councils. They had crossed the gorge on the symbolic bridge, and traversed the northern face of the great mountain. Yet somehow, they stood empty handed, alone in the summit room.

Unable to handle the pressure of searching any longer, Amir removed the final match from his pocket. He struck the tip against the side of the tiny box, and let the flicker become a flame. Holding the scroll in his left hand and the match in his right, he put them together and lit the bottom right corner of the ancient parchment.

Eva tried to snatch it away, but he dropped the match and held the scroll out of her reach. The match burned out harmlessly on the floor as Eva fell to his feet in despair. He held the burning map in his outstretched arm as he stood by the wall of encircling glass. Then, when he looked down into Eva's eyes, he noticed a new look on her face. It was not a look of despair... but of hope.

Her hand reached slowly toward the sky as her eyes widened with sudden understanding. Amir's eyes followed her now extended finger to the upper portion of the map on the scroll. Their final clue had been in their pockets since the beginning of the journey.

He quickly extinguished the flaming edge and held the map against the glass wall. Eva stood beside him and stared at the symbol. The sunlight shined in from the west, illuminating the parchment from behind. In the painted sky over their symbolic map, The Vitruvian Man appeared within the outline of the sun. Illuminated by the light of the world, the image hovered over the summit of the great mountain. The eclipse had finally passed, and they understood.

Always close, but so extremely hard to find. *The secret treasure literally existed within us,* they thought. *The answers to life's deepest concerns were concealed by our nature to look for happiness in other things.*

The knowledge of how to unite the world was metaphorically written into their genetic code, and could be learned by studying the human body as a living analogy of the bigger picture. No wonder the mysterious woman had gone to such lengths to show them the way; it was the destiny of all mankind.

"And to think," said Amir, "We doubted her until the very end of our journey. Imagine how much stress we could have avoided by just trusting her from the start."

"Ah," said a familiar female voice from behind them, "had you never made the journey, you would never have believed."

Amir and Eva turned in surprise to see the woman standing in the center of the table. Tears welled up in Amir's eyes, as he recognized her face. For the first time in many years, he saw his mother Nadia. A blue surgical mask hung from her neck as she smiled back. Her little boy had returned, just as The Great Mystery had promised.

CHAPTER
38

While the excitement of realizing the location of the secret treasure was quite intense, it lasted for only a moment before reality set back in. Following a warm embrace between Amir and his mother, he looked around and asked her a question.

"Where's dad?" he asked, expecting to have seen him as well.

"Your father cannot wait to see you," explained Nadia, "but you've only figured out half of the puzzle. You must finish the quest."

Though they knew the location of the treasure, they did not possess the knowledge to use it. The scientific council had vanished, and taken their videos with them. Without some kind of reference, they would never convince others to see from the same unique perspective. Without proof, they could not unite the world.

Fortunately, Eva knew exactly where the remainder of their missing knowledge would be. It was just a matter of how to access it. She led Amir down the stairs while Nadia remained in the upper room, staring out at the kingdom she so desperately wanted to save.

As they approached the base of the stairs Amir realized what Eva was thinking. Just minutes earlier, Amir had gotten frustrated at the fading image instead of noticing what was actually happening. Whether by anger or by peace, one discovers the same truth.

The passing sun above had caused an eclipse of the shadowy image on the floor. *Whoever built this room was a genius*, thought Amir. *No one would recognize the symbol's significance without knowing Leonardo himself.* His Vitruvian Man had been intended to lead seekers to the treasure's enduring location. However, it could not reveal the key for using it.

In fact, the idea of a "universal man" had been around for centuries, yet its powerful significance had remained unnoticed. Since the idea first appeared, people had been too preoccupied to look beneath the surface.

At the bottom of the stairs, Eva and Amir stared at the floor, not seeing anything but the cold marble.

"We have to be missing something," Eva said. "I just can't put my finger on it."

"Maybe there's a button or something," he suggested. "How did you open this room in the first place?"

"I didn't," Eva explained, "Isaac did."

CHAPTER
39

Eva ran her fingers across the smooth marble floor. She felt for clues, which might now be invisible in the dimly lit room. At first, she was disappointed, but then something caught her attention. There on the dark surface, at the outer edge of where the image had been, she found a small indent in the cold stone.

It wasn't much, but upon further inspection, she discovered three more similar areas. Each was spaced evenly around the outer edge of the previously visible circle.

Amir pressed on one of the indentations, but it did not budge. Eva tried another, and another, but had the same results. She was about to give up, but Amir insisted that they try something else.

"Let's try pressing on all four at the same time," he suggested. "You press on those two where the hands are, and I'll press on these two by the feet."

He placed his thumbs on the small squares and waited for Eva to get hers set in place. They hovered over their hands to get maximum pressure as they pushed. Eva counted, "On three," she said. "One...two...three..."

As they pressed, the circular marble slab rose slightly from the surrounding floor. The tense silence in the room was briefly interrupted by the hiss of escaping air, finally freed from the hidden compartment beneath. Amir and Eva's eyes locked on to one another. They knew they had found something important.

Unsure of how to lift the heavy panel of marble, they felt around the outer edge of the raised circle. Corresponding to the location of the indentations, four handles had been carved into the stone's edge. Each was cut deep enough for good grips during lifting.

All that remained was removing the cover, and discovering the secret that lay hidden inside.

Amir grabbed on to two of the handles, and Eva grabbed the others. She counted to three once again... and the panel lifted with ease.

CHAPTER
40

Eva and Amir placed the circular marble slab on the floor beside the compartment. The opening was surprisingly shallow, and the contents looked very familiar. Inside the small compartment was a single, dusty, leather-bound book. On the cover was a raised circular image, a symbol that Amir knew very well.

The design on the cover was unlike any of the sacred books they had lost earlier on their trip. On the other hand, the book was of the same superb quality, and someone had surely gone to great lengths to protect it. For what it seemed, the wise men at the temple had been unwilling to offer this special book as part of their test.

Eva reached down and wiped the dust away from the dark-blue cover, revealing the great detail of the symbolic emblem. To her surprise, it was not The Vitruvian Man. What she saw instead was an Eagle, displayed in a very similar position. A shield of stars and stripes covered its torso, while its wings and feet stretched toward the outer edges of the circle. In one claw, the eagle grasped an olive branch... in the other, the arrows of war.

Overhead was a smaller cloud-like circle containing thirteen stars, reminding them momentarily of their lesson at the symbolic bridge. But despite the stars, it was something else that finally caught Amir's attention. On a scroll held tightly in the eagle's mouth, was the Latin phrase, E PLURIBUS UNUM.

"This is it," Amir confirmed, "I think we found it."

He reached down to pick up the ancient book. Upon reading the phrase, Amir's life of learning as a young boy passed before him in a flash. He remembered the stories his mother and father had told him about the great nation from which his ancestors had come. He remembered the dire circumstances, which had led them to change their ways.

Their intentions had been good, but their careless way of living was adopted by many others. The power and prestige of the United States attracted many followers, but those nations failed to realize one very important thing. The material wealth of the young nation far outweighed their collective wisdom.

He explained the story to Eva as best as he could before removing the book.

"In the end, a great book emerged from within the United States. Its purpose was to unite the world, and save their planet from destruction. Though they could not save the Earth, they took to the skies in search of a new beginning. What we've discovered here my friend... is their book."

Eva slowly removed it from the compartment. She opened the cover, and noted the image on the title page. The Vitruvian Man hovered above the book's title, *The Great Mystery: A Guide for Human Progress.*

They had clearly found what they were looking for. While no author was listed, it did note that the compilation of wisdom had been compiled from many sources within the famed Library of Congress.

They sat happily on the cold marble floor, entranced by the power of what they had found. As they flipped through the many pages, they realized the complexity of the book. It contained excerpts from many of the lost sacred texts, artwork from numerous eras, and spectacular color images portraying human anatomy, physiology, and psychology.

The book was broken down into chapters, each bearing the title of a major body system. Each system was related to humanity as a whole, and how the species worked just like a single body: The Vitruvian, or Universal Body.

The intent of the authors was clear; the secret treasure for uniting the world was analogous with the workings of the human body itself. In the very first pages, it described how each individual person was simply a cell within the larger human race. Each performed its own specific jobs, but was only valuable if their work supported the whole.

Over time, the human race had evolved from an infant-like state into a reckless teenager, and from there they had grown up. The goal, it seemed, was to be like a wise elder: fully aware of itself and its relation to the rest of the universe. Eva and Amir had found the guide for bringing mankind into a new revelation. They had found the great perspective, and the key to unlocking human potential. *E PLURIBUS UNUM*, as the seal on the book's cover reminded them...*Out of Many, One*.

Eva handed the book to Amir, and he flipped through a few of the thin gold leaf pages. As Eva looked around for anything they might have missed, she startled him with yet another discovery.

"Look!" she exclaimed. Pointing toward the bottom of the compartment, she drew his attention away from the book to place where it once sat. The great seal was carved into a small circle in the center of the compartment's base. The image was slightly raised, and Eva knew exactly what it was. They had found their way out.

CHAPTER
41

Eva held her breath as she pressed the button. Initially, nothing happened, and she wondered if the function might have been disabled. Then, a familiar sound traveled from the next room over. The elevator had arrived, and the doors were open.

Together, they slid the marble cover back over the secret compartment. Amir held the book in his arms, certain they had found what the old woman had promised. They walked toward the elevator, and approached the open doors. In the next room over, Nadia had descended the stairway, and was waving goodbye.

"Are you coming with us?" Amir asked.

"Go ahead," his mother replied. She was confident that her son had now found his way. "I'll be down in a little while."

"Okay mom," replied Amir, sounding a bit sad as they backed into the elevator. "I'll see you soon."

As the doors closed behind them, Eva reached to press the button for the lobby. She could picture Amir's father waiting downstairs, anxious to congratulate him on a successful journey. However, she didn't understand why Nadia had chosen to remain behind. Such an event was surely a family affair.

As she reached for the elevator button, Amir grabbed her hand before she could press it. Eva was surprised by his sudden hesitation to go on. She looked into his glazed eyes, and found him on the verge of tears. His grin grew into a full smile as he gently pulled her hand away from the button, never letting go.

"What is it?" Eva asked. "Is everything ok?"

Amir was filled with excitement, knowing that the two of them would finally unite the world. With a calm voice, barely hinting at his actual emotion, he answered.

"We're not going to the lobby just yet."

Amir reached with his left hand and activated the digital map on the elevator's rear wall. The large three-dimensional color display came to life once again. A reddish glow indicated their location near the top level of the mountain fortress. Amir stared at the map for a moment, then back at Eva.

"Where else would we go?" Eva asked. "Don't you want to see your father?"

"Of course I do," answered Amir, as he pressed his finger to an area of the map that appeared to be nothing but dense rock.

According to the display, four stories of solid granite were all that separated the summit chamber from the lobby down below. With the exception of the elevator shaft, nothing else was there.

"What are you doing?" Eva questioned. "There's nothing ..."

Eva stopped short of finishing her sentence as the password entry window popped up on the map display.

Why would it request a password for an area that doesn't exist, she wondered.

"As a guardian of the secret treasure," Amir said softly, "you'll need to become familiar with the vault."

CHAPTER
42

Every great treasure is kept in a special place. Stockpiles of gold and rare jewels were stored in ancient underground tombs all over the world. Mother Nature herself even hid her precious diamonds deep within the planets. The secret guide for a peaceful humanity was no different. It was hidden within our very selves, a place we rarely look for help. It was truly an intelligent design.

With the secret treasure written into our DNA, it would always be close by, but hard to find. Our selfish human nature drives us to seek it, yet only by working together, and learning to depend on one another, can anyone find the time to make such a profound scientific discovery.

Even a surgeon, who has studied the inner workings of the body, and seen the details of the great design first hand, rarely notices the larger implications. Only a seeker, looking in the right place, for the right reasons, can realize it. The greatest treasure ever known, has been hiding in plain sight since we first asked, *why*?

Like any good vault, access required a unique password. It had been chosen so that only the wise could enter, and discover the knowledge that would lead the human race to their fullest potential. In addition, this vault only allowed one attempt. If the right password was entered, that person's fingerprints were scanned and saved, thereby giving them access forever. On the other hand, a single wrong entry would inhibit them from ever approaching the mountain complex again.

"So," Amir said to Eva in anticipation, "let's see what you've got."

Eva stared at the screen, unsure of what he thought she knew. Then Amir took out the book and gave it to her as a hint.

Immediately, she began to type. She tapped the letters on the touch screen keypad one at a time until she had spelled out the book's title: *The Great Mystery*. However, as she attempted to submit the password for approval, Amir stopped her once again.

Having descended from the Guardians, Amir had learned Latin as a young boy. It wasn't until seeing the symbol on the guidebook that he realized why the ancient

Roman script had been so carefully preserved within the family circle.

He desperately wanted Eva to figure it out for herself and enjoy the thrill of the greatest treasure hunt known to mankind.

"Think about it for a moment," He suggested. "What's unique about the book?"

Eva thought about the knowledge contained in the book. It all seemed unique considering what it meant. At first, she struggled to pick out a single word or phrase. If anything, she thought it had to be the title. Then it hit her like a bolt of lightning, and she knew.

Amir smiled as Eva closed the book and stared at the Latin inscription on the scroll held within the eagle's mouth. *Now we're on track,* he thought.

Eva recognized the phrase as the only part of the book, or of any language she had ever seen, which was not written in English. Though she had no idea what it meant, she did recognize the rarity and uniqueness of the script. She glanced at Amir quickly, acquiring his apparent approval, and then typed the phrase on the touch pad... *E PLURIBUS UNUM...*

Amir was thrilled. Eva submitted the password and watched anxiously as it was accepted. The elevator slowly descended three stories, and then stopped. When the doors opened, a wall of thick steel, similar to the one they had encountered on the trail, stood in their way. A small rectangular screen was located in the center of the fortified door.

The second password was an additional safeguard, ensuring that one person could never enter the vault alone. Though the entry code was different than the first, it would not seem so to a true Guardian.

Amir placed his hand on the display, and it came to life. The system immediately recognized his prints, and connected him to a family from the internal database. He was permitted a single attempt.

A similar touch pad keyboard appeared, and requested his password entry. Amir thought briefly about the magnitude of what he and Eva were about to complete. The entire key for implementing their secret treasure was contained within the ancient Latin phrase. It was that simple, yet powerful perspective that was necessary to unite the world, or any small group for that matter. Amir breathed slowly and confidently as he entered the English translation...*OUT OF MANY...ONE.*

He held his breath...and submitted his entry. Amir and Eva watched as the sealed door hissed, and rose into the ceiling. The vault was open. Light shined in from the stained glass ceiling above, illuminating the most magnificent room in the complex.

Amir and Eva stared in awe as their eyes surveyed the marvelous domed chamber. The windowless vault was filled to the brim with the priceless treasures of ancient America. Floor to ceiling mahogany shelves contained thousands of books, chronicles of the human mind, each neatly organized like the chapters of their newfound guidebook.

A large colorful tile mosaic covered the center of the white marble floor. They instantly recognized the circular design as The Great Seal of the United States of America.

As the soon to be world leaders walked toward the center of the room, they were startled by a strange rattling noise in the empty elevator to their rear. Before they could even react, a rush of blustery cold wind swept in through the open doors as if the elevator were a window to the icy world outside. They shielded their eyes until it calmed just seconds later.

When they uncovered their faces, The Great Mystery was hovering slightly above the floor in the center of the room. It seemed that it was time for their final encounter. Soon, the world would be theirs.

CHAPTER
43

Amir and Eva had journeyed from afar for this very moment. While they began in doubt regarding the promises of the old woman, their experience had transformed their doubt into mere certainty. One by one, her promises had come to pass, and the inevitable climax of their epic journey was just moments away. Soon, they would unite the world; not by offering something new, but by revealing what had always been.

The Great Mystery hovered silently in the center of the cavernous room. Having previously been awed by the deity's mysterious attributes, Amir and Eva felt they would have been prepared for the final encounter. Nevertheless, something was amiss, and they could feel it.

The mysterious old woman, having always been a different but very real looking creature, seemed transparent in the secret library. Her ghostlike appearance revealed yet another aspect of her endless possibilities.

Amir and Eva moved in for the conversation, but each was startled when their once invincible protégé showed her first signs of vulnerability. Their faith shook as her words crackled like static in the air. The sound came from here and there, but not all at once like it had before. Neither of the young guardians could understand what was being said.

"Something's not right," Amir said to Eva from behind.

The hovering woman let out another broken whisper, and then began to flicker. Eva was now standing close enough to touch her, but until then she never had the courage to do so. However, having witnessed the sudden flickering and stuttering, she was much less impressed than she had been as a child. She carefully reached out her left hand to touch the shoulder of the mysterious ghost.

Eva let out a gasp as her hand effortlessly pierced the torso of the strange imposter. Reflexively, she pulled her hand back, but the woman never even flinched. Suddenly unable to speak, Eva stepped forward fearlessly, moving right through the transparent creature. Though her belief in The Great Mystery had been a long work in progress, it faded a thousand times faster. She had been tricked by an advanced holographic technology, and she knew it. She felt betrayed, and somewhat hopeless. What had once seemed a miracle in her primitive hometown, was now much less impressive. Within the confines of the great mountain fortress, even the impossible could be explained. *What else is there to believe in*, she thought.

As Eva's faith faded into nothing, so too did the ghost. It flickered a few more times, just toying with her primitive mind...then vanished into thin air.

Eva looked back at Amir near the elevator doors. Tears were welling up in her eyes. He walked over to comfort her with an embrace. Holding her tightly, he calmly whispered a single question into her ear.

"Why are you crying?" he asked. "We'll be fine."

But Eva did not answer.

"I'm disappointed as well," Amir continued, "but we must move on. I'll bring you home now if you wish. Just tell me what's wrong."

Eva sobbed on his shoulder, momentarily unable to answer the question. Then, after a moment of hesitation, she answered with true sadness and disappointment.

"I only wanted to unite the people of the world," she said. "Think of the suffering we could have eased if all people really were one, and they knew it. I thought we had that power within our grasp, and now it's gone. It all seemed so real. I really thought we would do something great with our lives."

"You are a good person Eva," replied Amir. "But we must accept this great deception and move on. Perhaps we can find another treasure."

"I could not care less about treasure Amir," Eva answered feeling somewhat insulted. "My tears are for those who try, but suffer due to the lack of unity in the world. My tears are for those who feel alone, when such a thought is so far from the truth. The secret book still makes sense to me, but I don't know how we can accomplish such a daunting task without the help of The Great Mystery."

Now sure that Eva was worthy of Guardianship, Amir answered.

"Have no fear my friend, The Great Mystery is very real. We simply exist within it, not apart from it. Because of its perfect design, there is no need for outside intervention. That is what people like you and I are here for. All one must do is discover this, and act in accordance with that great discovery. We are not merely alive, but the Guardians of Life itself. The ability to learn, acknowledge, and embrace this fact is what separates humans from other species. We must make the choice. We must release our attachment to the delusion of independence, and embrace our true place within the Universal Body, that of The Great Mystery."

Eva wasn't sure what to think. It sounded good, but she had been tricked once before on this journey and had no desire to let that happen again. She needed more than words to get her believing again. As she stood there thinking in silence, Amir knew it was time.

He offered his last hope for saving Eva's faith in the mission.

"I would like to introduce you to my father."

CHAPTER
44

Eva wasn't quite sure how meeting Amir's father would help with their quest. They did still have the secret book, but its power was based on the promises of The Great Mystery. While she could accept that such power could come from a mysterious deity, she somehow could not see it in herself.

Eva, like many others, had been conditioned to look for help in the heavens, while the awesome power for change lay dormant just beneath the surface of her own skin. Such belief had been her source of hope throughout the journey, and had given her the courage and desire to go so far.

"Where is your father now?" she asked.

"He's here," replied Amir.

A look of confusion swept over Eva's face as he anxiously walked over to the bookshelves and scanned for a particular volume. He seemed to know exactly the section, but had a bit of trouble pinpointing its precise location. Finally, he stopped.

Eva scanned the other books in his immediate vicinity. To her astonishment, the sacred books from the temple were all there, neatly organized on the shelves. Though one seemed to be missing, she was dumbfounded as to where they had come from. She had witnessed the books being stolen with her own eyes, and seen the suffering caused by their own incompetence at the inn.

"I thought the books had been destroyed," she said with confusion in her voice. "The ones we lost at the inn were one of a kind, right?"

"Things are rarely what they seem," he explained. "The sacred books are but one path to the treasure. They are not the only path to happiness. What would become of the young peasant girl who could not read, had books been your only hope? Did you not find your treasure despite your illiteracy?"

Eva could see his point, but was still unsure of certain things.

"The books are windows to the soul. They are a given culture's guide for experiencing the divine, and promoting unity within a society. Each should be cherished and preserved based on the immense good that they have promoted within the world."

"So why are these good books so dangerous?" she asked. "Those wars on the mountainside nearly decimated half of our world."

"Nearly," Amir replied, "but you'll notice that natural laws have a unique way of eliminating those who constantly act in opposition to their own best interest. That's why we must share the secret treasure of *The Great Mystery*. Once people understand how we are all connected to one another, they will unite as promised, and work together for the common good."

"But the sacred books have existed for a long time, and the people have not united," Eva said. "What's so different about this new book? How will we unite so many people?"

"Quite simply," Amir replied, "we won't. The truth will unite the people, not us. When they see that they are all connected in this way, they will learn to make choices accordingly. We do not need to teach people right and wrong. We only need to teach them to identify with the whole, as opposed to their individual selves. That is why our book is different. It is about identity, not judgment."

"So you're saying that we will not be judged?" Eva asked, noting the stark contradiction to many of the other sacred books. "Surely, this theory will not be accepted among the people."

"We are all judged Eva, but the process of Justice is much simpler than we imagine. It is served on a continuing basis, through the natural laws of cause and effect. It is applied not to individuals, but to humanity as a whole. Though a man might escape the consequences of his actions, mankind will not. This is just another example of why we must think of ourselves as a universal body. It is reality, and by not accepting it, we only hurt ourselves.

"If you wish to know the difference between right and wrong, ask this one simple question: Will my actions support the well being of humanity? Rarely must we consider it further than this. For today you may find yourself in good fortune, tomorrow your fate may depend on the good fortune of others.

"Having discovered the secret treasure, we will surely be held accountable for what we do with this powerful knowledge. It is not possible, or even necessary, to rid the world of suffering. The world will only be united through balance, and the avoidance of all extremes."

Eva understood what they had to do, but she couldn't imagine a world without a powerful deity that stood up for right, and intervened for a chosen few. However, a flash from the past gave her the hope she had been looking for.

The Sun may not rise and fall as you once thought, Mr. Einstein had said, *but it does exist.*

Amir turned back to the empty space on the shelf where he had paused just moments ago. A few books were tipped slightly leaning on the ones to the left. He stood them upright and stared into the dark gap. He turned to look at Eva as he reached into the empty space, and felt along the back of the shelf. Just as his father had told him, the button was there.

"Now it's time for our final encounter," Amir said.

As he pressed the button, the sound of escaping air filled the cavernous library. Eva and Amir turned instinctively toward the sound, and watched as the large tile emblem slowly lifted from the floor. Fluorescent lights glowed from within the rising chamber.

Amir had anxiously waited for this moment for many years. He would soon be with his father, once again.

CHAPTER
45

As the apparent command center lifted slowly from beneath the floor, it became even more spectacular to Eva. She had never before seen such a bizarre place. There were buttons, levers, lights of every color, and video monitors all throughout the room.

Finally, the upward movement ceased, and the steam dissipated into the air. As the fog lifted, the glowing lights seemed to dim. A thick glass door slid open, and there he was.

Amir could not believe his eyes. He had not seen his father in many years, but did not remember him being so old. In fact, the man who emerged from the chamber looked completely unfamiliar, and Amir instantly developed an uneasy feeling in his gut.

As the man walked slowly toward them, his green eyes continued to glow like the lights within the chamber. He stopped, and raised his long arms up from his sides.

"Welcome home children," he said. "My name is Enoch."

Enoch was not Amir's father. Something was wrong. He did not remember anyone other than his parents having access to this room, or the command center. He tried to hide his disappointment, but Enoch saw right through his disguise.

"Is there a problem Amir?" asked the old man.

But Amir could not answer. He remained silent as the lump in his throat dissolved. As he looked on, he could not understand what he saw.

Eva, on the other hand, recognized the man immediately. She curiously walked over to verify her assumption, and validate her belief once again. She touched his face with her hands and felt his aging skin. She searched for something, anything that would give her confirmation.

Finally, she stared into his bright green eyes and waited. Chills ran through her veins as the feeling of excitement boiled inside, waiting to erupt at any moment.

She stared into the old man's soul: and suddenly realized that it was not separate from her own...and then it happened. His green eyes glowed noticeably brighter for only a second, and then returned to normal, just as quickly and effortlessly as they had changed.

At that point, Eva knew. She backed off, and stood by Amir as she awaited the imminent conversation.

"Do you know him?" Amir asked.

"I'm surprised you don't," she replied. "Why are you acting so tense?"

She still doesn't understand, thought Amir. *We are the chosen ones because my parents are the last of the Guardians. This Enoch has nothing to do with it.*

As far as he knew, his mother and father had been calling the shots all along. While Eva had learned to believe in the unknown, and to trust in The Great Mystery, Amir did not see such things as necessary. People had always worshiped the unknown, but in his world, everything could be explained. There were no miracles, just science.

"This man is not my father," he explained. "I don't know how he got here, or what he did with my dad, but this is not him. He cannot be trusted."

"Amir," replied Eva, "I don't think you understand. It's *him*."

"No it isn't!" he shouted with confidence. "Just trust me! I would know him if I saw him."

Suddenly, Enoch interrupted their conversation. "Is that so?" he asked. He held his hands together behind his back as his arms hung to his sides. "It seems you aren't as good at recognizing things as you may think."

His surprisingly stern tone caught Amir by surprise. Perhaps he had mistaken the man's identity.

I guess it's possible, he thought, *but highly unlikely*.

"Tell me then," he said to Enoch. "Where is my father now?"

Eva awaited the answer just as anxiously as Amir. She knew exactly who Enoch was, but the well-being of her friend's father was equally important.

Enoch then replied in an eerily familiar whisper, "Amir, you have gone to great lengths to lead this woman here. You have taught her life's most valuable lessons. You have led her to what you know to be the greatest, and most powerful treasure in the universe. Yet you have no idea who I am?"

"I want to know where my father is," he said. "If he is gone then I am in command here. I was next in line to rule the world. All I needed was a partner, and I have found one."

"Did you say *rule*?" asked Enoch. "Whatever happened to *unite*? You were to unite the world, not rule it. You have failed to learn a vital lesson my son: That no one person is above the rest. We're all susceptible to suffering, and more so when we do not act in accordance with the well being of the whole. Have you become so lost in your own agenda that you have forgotten your part? Do not overestimate your worth apart from The Great Mystery, for there is none. You play your part or you don't, then you die. Does your own body not go on despite the loss of a single cell? You know this, yet have failed to see this principle in life itself. Now pay attention."

Amir realized he had gone off track with his priorities, but had no idea what Enoch was about to reveal.

"When you were a child, your father and I were great friends. We spoke nearly every day. He was one of the finest Guardians the world has ever known. Nevertheless, he was faced with a great challenge. His only child, an adopted young boy, had an enlarged heart, and needed surgery."

"I know about my heart Sir," Amir replied. "I had my valve replaced when I was young, and I just had it done again recently. Tell me something I don't know."

"Well," replied Enoch in a calm, but authoritative voice, "if you'll listen, I will."

Amir felt a rush of embarrassment flow over himself as he realized that he had lost self-control. "My apologies," he said. "Please continue."

"A valve alone may save you now, but this was not the case when you were a child," explained Enoch. "At that time, you required a new heart. Your father was the one with the valve problem."

"I don't understand," he said. "I just had my valve replaced the other day."

"Exactly." Enoch replied, giving Amir a few seconds to grasp what was being explained to him. "Without you, the line of Guardians would have ended, and your father could not let that happen. Your father arranged to have his own heart removed and given to you, he then followed through without hesitation. Before he died however, he devised a plan to prepare you for the job, while preventing you from feeling responsible for his death."

Amir and Eva were awed by the sacrifice of the great man. He had surely possessed the wisdom of the secret treasure.

"But he was with me in the village by the river," explained Amir. "He taught me everything I know."

"Did he?" asked Enoch rhetorically. "It is often hard to pinpoint who taught us the things we know. We often put the pieces together in a way that is most pleasing to us. However, such shortcuts rarely lead to the truth.   We must be concerned with the entire story, and avoid being consumed by a single part.   The truth exists only in the whole, and deception in anything less."

Enoch's voice returned to a more natural sound.

"Your father saved your life by giving up his own. He gave up his time for the sake of you, so that his example might remain etched in your mind forever.   Through similar unselfish behavior, anyone can help to unite the world."

Eva realized what he meant. The world did not need a ruler. It needed individuals to simply act in accordance with humanity's best interest. A healthy body consisted of healthy cells, and it was the same with the human race. The people needed the secret treasure, not just the leaders.

"While sacrifice may be difficult for the individual," continued Enoch, "it benefits the Universal Self, and makes us all stronger. This is the measure of an honorable life. Imagine a world where this was the collective mindset.   Unity would be unavoidable.

"Action is the language by which all people communicate with one another. Mere words are useless in the pursuit of a peaceful world."

The speech was moving on, but Amir was still confused.

"If my father had a bad heart," he asked, "why would he give it to me?"

"Your father gained his wisdom by confronting the idea of death," explained Enoch. "His condition forced him to consider it every day.

"He possessed a strong heart with a small, but significant valve problem. Yet the value of his priceless gift was not the heart itself, but its defect. For he knew that it would drive you to understand the meaning of life. What you saw as a defect, he saw as your teacher.

"Your father was a great man, and that part of him still exists... within you."

Amir's hope had been restored, and he was ready to get on with the day. He and Eva stared into Enoch's bright green eyes, and wondered what was next.

"So then," Amir inquired, "if you are not my father, are you The Great Mystery?"

"No more than you," replied Enoch, "no more than you."

Suddenly, the room began to tremble.

CHAPTER
46

Amir and Eva looked up at the magnificent stained glass window high above, and watched as it cracked, and then shattered. Pieces began to break loose and fall from the ceiling. As the walls shook, thousands of books made their way toward the edge of the shelves. One by one, they fell to the floor.

"What's going on?" yelled Amir. His voice was barely audible over the noise of the earthquake.

"We must get out of here," replied Enoch, his eyes no longer glowing. "Hurry, get into the chamber."

"Shouldn't we take the elevator?" asked Eva loudly. "There's an escape from the lobby. That's how I got in."

Just then, Amir remembered his mother Nadia, who was still trapped on the top floor. There was no time to save her. He hoped she knew another way out.

"Send the elevator up," said Enoch. "Then come with me. If she's up there, she can use it to escape."

Amir did as he was told. He typed in the passwords and jumped out as the doors closed. The elevator was on its way up, and they were stuck in the library, awaiting their demise.

The violent tremble of the earthquake increased tenfold. They followed Enoch into the command center. The doors closed, and it descended into the floor.

Eva was curious of the room's purpose. As the chamber descended slowly, she asked Enoch about its use.

"What is this room for?" she asked.

"It's for those who don't yet believe," he replied.

Eva did not understand, and was unsure of how they would escape.

Enoch explained as he manned the controls.

"The secret treasure is something that everyone searches for. This command center helps people find it. Though you discovered the old woman to be a holographic human deception, it did not change the powerful nature of your secret treasure. Did it?"

"No," she said, "I guess not."

"Then think of this machine as our version of the sacred books. We've created a virtual experience: a lens through which one might discover the secret treasure much faster than they otherwise would."

Enoch turned to face a frightened Amir. "Your father chose me to look after you," he said. "I'm doing the best I can."

"So you aren't The Great Mystery?" Amir asked.

"You may see The Great Mystery in what I have done, but it is not me. I am simply a cell in that body, just like you, and every step brings us closer to our imminent destiny: The realization of where, and who, we've always been. This is the final revelation.

"While one man can take a step, he cannot endure the journey alone, for walking the path is a collective journey. When we reach our destination, it will happen again. It is the heartbeat of the Universe, and the true realm of eternity."

The chamber stopped... and the doors opened. To the surprise of Amir and Eva, they were in the same lobby where Eva first got on the elevator to go to the summit meeting room. The book on the table was gone. Nadia was not there.

"Follow me!" said Enoch, as the mountain continued to tremble. "We must leave before the eruption!"

CHAPTER
47

They raced down the halls as the windows to the outside cracked. From what they could see, the sky was darkening with smoke, and the sun was hardly visible through the dark clouds overhead. Knowing it would be impossible to escape, but feeling impelled to try, they rushed for the doors to the trail outside.

"Why did you bring us here if the whole place was going to blow?" Amir yelled at Enoch over the mountain's terrifying grumble. "I don't understand why we went to all the trouble. What good is the treasure if our kingdom is destroyed?"

Enoch stopped at the door leading outside and punched in the password. The heavy steel door slowly began to rise. He answered Amir's question as they waited for it to open.

"This is not over! You must escape and tell the world of the secret treasure! Now come on! Let's go!"

The door opened, and the smoky outside air came rushing into their uninviting lungs. They mounted the three horses awaiting them near the entrance, and rode fast across the melting north face of the trembling mountain. All around, the landscape crumbled. Fire came up from the land as molten lava spewed from the vents of the super volcano upon which they rode.

They could no longer see the summit, but could hear the eroding complex as it collapsed upon itself. They rode down the path as fast as they could, reaching the bridge in a matter of minutes. They dismounted their horses, knowing the fragile bridge would never hold the added weight.

Perhaps it would hold long enough for them to run across on foot. Amir and Eva looked back at Enoch, knowing the bridge was their only escape.

How did he keep up during the frantic escape? Eva wondered.

Yet he had stayed with them every step of the way. In fact, he had even remained calm, guiding them out in the process.

"Where do you get such endurance at your age?" she asked. "You must be nearly one hundred years old."

To her surprise, Enoch answered, "I would be inclined to ask the same question of you my friends. Perhaps next time you'll be more careful of what you chase in life, for there's no turning back when it's all over."

Amir and Eva suddenly looked at each other, and realized that they had aged many years on their trip down the mountain. Their hair had turned white, their skin had wrinkled, and their once strong limbs seemed thin and fragile.

"This is not fair! What will happen to our secret treasure?" Amir asked, suddenly feeling his power slip away. "There will be no kingdom to unite when this is over."

"There is always progress to be made," Enoch advised. "Pay attention to what you have learned, and never take a breath for granted. Now go! This bridge was not built for me."

"But what will we do?" asked Eva.

"You'll know when you get there," he replied.

Amir and Eva held hands and backed up toward the bridge's edge.

"Okay," Amir said, "thank you for everything. You're a great man!"

"Your father was a great man," Enoch replied.

"Perhaps," answered Amir with a wink as they moved out onto the trembling bridge, "But no more than you or I."

Enoch knew that Amir finally understood. He and Eva would be fine. His mission had been a success, and Amir's father would have been proud.

Amir removed the secret book from his coat and held it over his head for Enoch to see. "We'll see what we can do!"

As Amir and Eva began to run across the long bridge, pieces began to shake loose. Behind them, Enoch's bright green eyes illuminated yet again. He looked to the sky, and leapt for the stars, far beyond the smoke above.

Amir and Eva were midway across the bridge when it gave way. The pieces fell fast as the path beneath their feet disappeared. They ran and fell at the same time, aware that they would never reach the other side. They held tight to each other's hands as they fell with increasing speed. Their secret treasure would be lost forever. For the first time since meeting in the forest, fear encompassed the elder couple as their world quickly came to a violent end.

The great mountain erupted with a fury that had never been witnessed in all of human history. Fire and rock flew overhead as the Guardians fell into the deep, dark, endless gorge. The world collapsed upon itself, evaporating around them as they fell. They dropped right through the bottom of the gorge... straight through the planet... and into the deep dark realm of space.

The stars and planets imploded upon one another, and everything in existence was drawn back toward its origin. The Universe had completed another cycle of evolution, and like a beating heart, it prepared itself for yet another beat...

EPILOGUE

In a hospital room deep in the heart of Texas, The Great Seal of the United States of America adorned the gates outside the spectacular medical center in San Antonio. Within the magnificent fortress of compassion, The Great Mystery was at work yet again.

In a bed on the second floor intensive care unit, a young man was slowly awakening from the veil of anesthesia. He had been held motionless and unconscious for the past several hours while doctors, nurses, technicians, and others came together as a team to save his life. Having done this many times a day, they no longer saw the miraculous life changing power of what they were each taking part in.

For a moment, it seemed like they were back in the mountain complex, but it wasn't so. It was the fulfillment of the Guardians' greatest wish, the parts working together peacefully for the common good, evermore realizing their greatness as a larger entity.

As the young man slowly re-emerged from his slumber, he heard whispers coming at him from all around the room. Questions were being asked. Things were being said.

He could hear the voice of Enoch asking strange questions. He could hear the voice of Alexander advising someone nearby about the bridge to recovery. He could hear the voice of Aristotle, telling a loved one to remain patient, and understanding.

Then suddenly, he heard Eva...

Having been suddenly awakened by a frightening sense of falling through space, the young man opened his eyes for the first time since earlier that morning. His wife, friends, and family were by his side in the room, all the while ensuring that he was comforted in his time of great need. They were present because of a mysterious connection, and the pain was theirs as well.

The young man was hurting from his recent open-heart surgery, but was thankful to be safe from the imploding universe of his dream. He saw smiles all around the room, intertwined with looks of genuine concern. He realized that those in that room were his true friends. His wife held his hand as he smiled and drifted back to sleep.

That evening, as the visitors cleared the room, a surgeon carrying what appeared to be a very old anatomy textbook, quietly entered the patient's room. The young man's wife was fast asleep in an uncomfortable chair, never suspecting a thing as the mysterious person approached her husband's bedside. The surgeon placed her hand calmly on his shoulder, just enough to steal a moment of his much-needed rest.

Gradually, the soldier awakened, and opened his eyes. He was surprised to see the strange visitor standing by his side. The surgeon wore teal colored hospital scrubs, a white lab coat, and a badge with no picture or name. On the pocket of her coat, there was an embroidered design: the Great Seal of The United States of America. She spoke to the young man in a whisper, so as not to awaken his tired wife.

"How are you feeling?" asked the surgeon.

"I was better off asleep," replied the young man with a somewhat grumpy attitude. "It's the only way to forget the pain."

Being full of compassion, the surgeon did not wish to disturb the patient any further.

"I didn't mean to cause you suffering," replied the surgeon. "I will leave you alone.

I just wanted to check on you and make sure you were okay." She gave him a friendly smile of encouragement before preparing to exit the room.

"You take care of that beautiful family of yours," she said as her eyes began to glow in the dimly lit room. "A treasure like that is hard to find." Then, with a wink and a pat on the shoulder, she turned and left the room.

"Wait!" yelled the young man, startling his wife. "You forgot your..." He stopped short of finishing his sentence, unable to comprehend what lay beside him on the bed.

As he carefully picked up the ancient book, his heart rate increased in speed, causing the monitors to alarm. His wife jumped up and flipped on the lights just as the nurse came rushing in from the hallway. The young man quickly hid the book under the blankets and shielded his eyes from the bright lights overhead.

"Are you feeling alright?" asked the nurse.

He glanced around at the people entering his room, but was unable to find the mysterious surgeon.

"Did anyone see the woman who just left?" he asked. "It couldn't have been more than a minute ago."

The nurse was unsure of who the young man was referring to.

"The nurse's station is located right outside of your door sir. No one has come in or out of this room during the last half hour."

He thought briefly about asking more questions, but knew it would be to no avail.

"Never mind," he said as his pulse gradually slowed back within a normal range. "Perhaps I was dreaming again."

Having served as a nurse on the surgical ICU for many years, the caring professional did his best to calm the patient's fragile heart. He helped him settle back in, knowing that morning labs would be drawn in less than thirty minutes.

"Don't worry about a thing," he said. "Those strange dreams will go away after a week or so. The heart-lung machine can sometimes play tricks on the mind."

The young man smiled as the nurse turned off the lights and exited the room. When he was gone, the patient's wife moved closer to the bed. She held his hand, and leaned in to kiss his cheek.

"Are you sure everything's ok?" she asked, knowing that he probably would not admit it either way.

"I think I'll be just fine sweetheart," he answered.

"You don't seem certain," his wife replied. "Are the dreams so bad that you can't stand having them for another week?"

"Oh no," he answered, "it's not that at all. I only hope I can remember the one I just had."

"What was your dream about?" asked his exhausted best friend, who still had no idea what her husband now possessed.

"It's a long story," he said. "I'll tell you about it later. Let's just get some sleep while we still can. That stuff's hard to come by around here."

They exchanged smiles and began drifting back to sleep.

Deep within the young man's mind, he thought to himself as he lay in bed. *Many cells*, he had learned... *we are all but tiny cells in the body of The Great Mystery.*

He reached into the bedside cabinet and pulled out one of the sacred books. Flipping the pages, he arrived at a familiar verse, Mark 4.26-29. *A tiny seed*, he thought. *Could it really be true?*

As he began to close his eyes, he noticed the surgeon walking by the windows in the hall outside his room. She turned briefly, checking on her patient through the glass, and then moved down the hall. The soldier smiled to himself, knowing he would never be alone. *Only one person's eyes glow like that,* he thought. *No reason to make another scene of it.*

Long before sunrise on the following morning, the medical teams arrived to collect their data for another day of healing. As they entered the young couple's room, they were surprised to find them wide-awake, anxious to get on with the recovery, and with life.

Once again, the young man and his family stood at the foot of the great mountain. Together, they would set out on life's amazing journey... toward wherever their path may lead.

THE END

"The Kingdom of God is as if someone would scatter seed on the ground, and would sleep and rise night and day, and the seed would sprout and grow, he does not know how. The earth produces of itself, first the stalk, then the head, then the full grain in the head. But when the grain is ripe, at once he goes in with his sickle, because the harvest has come."

(Mark 4. 26-29)

The Great Mystery returns...

In this thought provoking follow-up to Slone's first allegorical masterpiece, *The Great Mystery*, we are once again reminded to slow down, and be inspired by life.

In an ongoing effort to shift our focus to a more interdependent reality, Slone uses this story to remind us of the world's most powerful, and universal law: "The Golden Rule."

Together in Paradise remains packed with the same adventure, intrigue, emotion, and wisdom that we have come to expect from this imaginative storyteller.

So, is heaven really some vaguely understood, and distant spiritual realm... or are we there already, on a global quest for the rediscovery of this perfect, and ancient truth?

Read for yourself, and decide.

CPSIA information can be obtained at www.ICGtesting.com
Printed in the USA
BVOW03s2031200615

405463BV00006BA/294/P